MYSTERY SHORT STORIES FOR KIDS PART II: A COLLECTION OF 20 PUZZLING, MYSTERIOUS DETECTIVE AND WHODUNNIT TALES FOR CHILDREN

MONSTER TALES, MISSING PLANETS, SPY ADVENTURES, MYSTERIOUS TOYS AND MORE

MYSTERY SHORT STORIES FOR KIDS

BOOK 2

JOHNNY NELSON

SILK PUBLISHING

1

WHO STOLE BILLY'S SMILE?

Charlotte and Billy loved playing games. They played together all the time. They loved exploring caves they found under the stairs. They fought aliens that lived in the lemon trees in their backyard.

Billy could always make Charlotte laugh. Billy put two lemons over his eyes and jumped out of the lemon tree. "Grumpledegoop is from Venus, and he has come to destroy your house," Billy yelled.

Charlotte would scream and run. "No! I shall trap and eat Grumpledogoop!"

They would play like this every day from the time they got home from school until they went to bed. On the weekends, they would play like this from the time they woke up until they went to bed. The only time they would stop would be when their mom called them to eat their meals or take a bath.

Charlotte and Billy were inseparable and loved each other very much. One Saturday, Charlotte woke up and bounced out of bed. She flung open Billy's door and found him still lying in bed. Charlotte jumped on the bed and shook Billy.

"Come on, Billy, let's go trap some aliens."

Billy rolled over onto his side and shrugged Charlotte off of him. "I don't feel like playing today, sorry."

"Are you sick?"

"I don't know. I just don't feel well. I want to go back to sleep."

Charlotte climbed off the bed and went to the kitchen. She went to the refrigerator and poured herself a glass of milk, and sat down at the table. It wasn't long before Charlotte's mom came into the kitchen.

"Well, Charlotte, I thought you and Billy would be outside fighting monsters."

Charlotte took a drink of milk and shrugged. "Billy says he didn't feel well and went back to sleep."

Mom frowned. "That isn't like Billy. I'll go check on him to see if I need to call Doc Martin."

Mom walked to Billy's room and found him curled on his side. She put her hand on his forehead. "Hey, Charlotte says you aren't feeling well. It doesn't feel like you are running a fever. Do you hurt anywhere?"

"No, I just don't feel good. I just want to sleep."

Mom frowned, bent down, and kissed him on the forehead. "Okay, I'll leave you alone, but you need to eat, so when I get breakfast cooked, I will bring you a plate."

"Okay, mom."

Mom left Billy's room and went back to the kitchen. Charlotte had drunk her milk and moved into the family room. She was sitting on a beanbag chair, reading a book.

Charlotte got through her first day without playing with her brother. She felt weird by the end of the day, like she had lost her best friend and she didn't know how to get him back.

This went on all weekend, and when Monday came around, Billy got up, got dressed, and walked to school with Charlotte. Charlotte tried to get him to play on the way to school, but he just kept telling her to leave him alone. Charlotte was very sad by the time they got to school. She went into her classroom, put her things away, and sat down at her desk. Her best friend at school walked up and asked her how her weekend was. Charlotte shrugged her shoulders and said boring.

"Are you feeling okay?" Mitzy asked.

"Not really, something is off with Billy, and I just don't know how to help him."

"Maybe he has a bug."

"I don't know, but I have to help him."

"We'll talk to him at recess together."

When recess rolled around, Mitzy and Charlotte found Billy sitting on a bench by himself.

"Hey, Billy, Mitzy is going to help us fight aliens today."

"I don't feel like fighting aliens."

"Why don't you feel like playing? Come on, Billy, you haven't played all weekend. If you tell us what's wrong, we might be able to help."

"I doubt it, by I have a big purple monster sitting on my back."

Charlotte looked behind Billy. "I don't see anything on your back."

"He's there; I can feel him. I have named him Simon."

"Simon must be grumpy and mean," thought Charlotte. "It seems as if he has swallowed Billy's smile."

Simon was always with Billy. One day, Charlotte just told Billy to just tell Simon to go away.

"Don't you think that I have tried that?" yelled Billy. "There are times that Simon feels like he is as big as a truck."

Billy gets angry at the silliest things most of the time now. Even when he eats, he chews like he is angry at his food.

One day, mom asks Billy to go for a walk with her. "I think the fresh air would do you some good."

Billy shrugged, "Fine, it won't help, but I'll go."

They walked together around the block. Mom smiled and waved at their neighbors, with Billy frowning and grumbling beside her. When they got back home, Billy stomped off to his bedroom and slammed the door.

There were days when Simon had such a hold on Billy that Billy couldn't get out of bed. Charlotte tried everything she knew to get Billy to fight off Simon.

"Come on, Billy, we have fought bigger monsters than this. You can do this. I know you can."

Billy would just shake his head and go to sleep.

Dad even tried to help Billy. One morning at breakfast, Billy was just picking at his food. Dad spoke up without putting his paper down. "If you would just eat better, you would feel better."

Billy tried to eat, but Simon would keep the food from going down. Billy got sadder and angrier as the days went by.

One day, Billy woke up, and Simon wasn't as big. Billy went running to Charlotte's room and woke her up. "Come on, let's play."

"Is Simon gone?"

Billy thought for a minute, "No, but he isn't as big today so let's play while we can."

Charlotte threw off the covers and got dressed. Billy was already in the backyard playing. Charlotte ran outside and began chasing Billy around the yard. It wasn't long before Billy got tired and had to sit down. Simon was back and kept Billy from playing.

Everybody had their own opinion of what was wrong with Billy and gave him advice on how to get rid of Simon. Billy tried everything that everyone told him, but nothing seemed to help. Charlotte tried everything she knew to distract Billy. She showed him her new book. She tried puzzles, games, and even her new train set, but nothing helped. Charlotte knew that Simon was making Billy angry and sad.

Charlotte had had enough of Simon. She was tired of Simon keeping Billy from playing and being happy. She grabbed a pillow and threw it at Simon. "Take that, Simon! You need to go away and give me my brother back!"

This made Billy smile, and Simon didn't feel so big. "Thanks, Charlotte."

Charlotte gave Billy a big hug, and Simon felt even smaller. Billy hugged Charlotte back, and Simon got a lot smaller.

When Billy's birthday rolled around, Charlotte helped mom bake him a cake. Billy blew out his candles and thanked his family. Billy smiles a little bit, and his smile is different, but at least he is smiling. Charlotte sat down beside Billy. "Is Simon making you sad today?"

"A little, I guess."

"But it's your birthday; won't he leave you alone just for today?"

"I want to be happy, but it is very hard for me to be happy with Simon around."

"How long do you think he is going to stay with you?"

"I don't know, but he makes me so tired."

Charlotte hugs Billy. "It's okay; we'll play on the days you feel like playing."

Billy was able to smile his old smile for the first time in a very long time. Simon got smaller.

Once Billy was brave enough to tell his family about Simon, the big purple monster, he began to feel better. Billy even got help from a friend of Doctor Martin's, Doctor Freedman. Doctor Freedman helped Billy talk about Simon and other things, and this made Simon get even smaller. Billy learned that anytime he was feeling sad or a bit off, talking to anybody helped him feel better. It was hard work, but Billy learned to trust his feelings, family, and friends and this kept Simon from controlling him. Billy is slowly getting his life back.

Billy and Charlotte got even closer because Charlotte never gave up on Billy even when he was at his worst. Charlotte knew her brother needed help, and she saw that she was the only one who was willing to fight Simon to get her brother back. Without Charlotte's help, Billy knew that he wouldn't have been able to fight off Simon, and he would have been at Simon's will for the rest of his life.

Simon is still there, and some days he is very large. These days, Charlotte just sits quietly beside Billy and gives him support if he asks. On most days, Simon is small and lets Billy and Charlotte have fun. These days, they fight off aliens in the lemon tree out back, or they hunt the things hiding in the cave under the stairs.

Charlotte helped Billy find his smile even though there are days when his smile isn't as bright as it used to be.

2

WHAT HAPPENED TO THE PATH?

Sabrina is a girl with long, auburn hair that goes all the way down her back. It has all the colors of autumn running through like deep reds and gold. Her eyes are as big and bright, and they are deep sea green. She is full of adventure and happiness. This is why she is so pretty; she shines from the inside, and it glows out into the world.

One afternoon, Sabrina decides to go on a walk. She fills a picnic basket full of goodies and begins skipping down the path into the woods behind her house. She begins skipping down the path and past all the familiar trees that are covered in bright, green leaves that are softly blowing in the wind. Sunshine is filtering through the leaves and making the grass look like a glowing carpet. Sabrina had promised her friends that she would pack all their favorite foods, and they would eat under the sunset.

The sunshine skips and bounces through the trees and kisses nature as it starts to wind down. It says good afternoon to the blue jays who sing good afternoon back. It says good day to the squirrels hunting nuts and acorns. It even says hello to the moon as it begins its climb into the big, blue sky.

Sabrina gets to her secret clearing right as the sun starts to sets. She begins unpacking all the food that she packed onto a huge, old tree stump. There is orange juice, strawberries with cream, carrots, rhubarb, pine nuts, pumpkin, and cherries. Sabrina sits down and waits for her friends. She is content watching the sun set and feeling it warming her face.

Her friends slowly begin arriving there Sammy the Squirrel, Greta the Groundhog, Richard the Rabbit, Oscar the Opossum, and Rita the Raccoon. Sabrina says good morning to her friends. Since her friends are nocturnal, they are just waking up to begin their day. They are soon seated around the stump and begin filling their empty tummies with all the wonderful food Sabrina has brought them. All the delicious food almost makes them fall asleep again. They lay back on the soft grass and watch the clouds float by as the sun finishes setting in the sky.

The friends try to see how many different things they can see in the clouds. Sabrina sees a dragon. Sammy sees an oak tree full of acorns. Richard sees a huge bunch of carrots. Greta sees a garden full of her favorite foods. Oscar sees another opossum. Rita sees a giant raccoon that fights evil.

The sky begins turning pink, and this makes the clouds turn into cotton candy. Then the sky turns to a soft violet. Sabrina's friends begin scurrying to wherever they go at night. They are happy and full. Sabrina is full of happiness and love and soon falls fast asleep, watching the clouds gently float by.

Sabrina suddenly wakes up and notices that the sun is sleeping and the moon is shining brightly. She looks around and notices that her surroundings look different. There are shadows everywhere, and everything has turned a soft blue color. The light coming from the stars and moon gives her skin a soft glow. She can hear birds fluttering overhead and crickets chirping nearby. She smells honeysuckle and jasmine in the air, and this helps bring Sabrina out of her slumber. She slowly gets up and stretches like a cat. She soon has her picnic basket packed, and she begins heading home.

Small white flowers are glowing in the clearing, swaying and dancing in the gentle breeze. Butterflies flutter in the breeze. They are as large as her hands. Their wings glow brightly in colors of fuchsia, orange, and gold.

Sabrina is thankful for this light as it will help her get home. She leaves her secret place and begins walking back through the forest. Everything is quiet, and she hears the wind rustling the leaves overhead and the wounds of the animals scurrying through the forest floor. Here and there, Sabrina sees golden eyes watching her through the leaves, but she isn't scared as she knows they belong to the owls.

Sabrina realizes she has walked for a very long time, and she stops to get her bearings. She realizes that she doesn't know how to get home now. She wonders who stole the path. She goes back the way she came to get back to her secret spot, but she soon finds herself in the middle of trees that she doesn't recognize. She takes a deep breath and keeps walking. She is trying to come up with a plan with every step she takes. She knows her friends live close by, and she can ask for their help. She takes the time to stop and look at the moon.

"Please, moon, help me get back home."

To Sabrina's surprise, the moon replied back, "To be like me, you have to look at the big picture."

Sabrina stands there looking up, waiting for more information. When nothing else came, she thanked the moon and continued walking. Soon, Sabrina sees a large patch of sky that is full of stars. She thinks, "the big picture."

"Hello, stars, will you help me?" Sabrina asks.

"We might be small, but we have a lot of light to give. With determination and lots of stars, we are able to give the world light. Even though it is dark, you need to continue shining your inner light."

"Thank you," says Sabrina.

Sabrina keeps walking and soon finds herself on the banks of the river. She is tired, and her feet hurt from all the walking. She doesn't have any idea what time it is, but she knows it is very late. The breeze is blowing harder here, and it blows through Sabrina's hair while cooling her cheeks. She looks across the river.

"Hello, river; it is so nice to meet you."

The river says hello back to Sabrina in a relaxed but soothing voice.

"I don't know how to get home. Can you help me?"

"Water can get through anything with a lot of persistence and patience."

"Well, thank you, river."

Sabrina takes her shoes off and places her feet in the cool water to soothe her feet. After some time, she gets up, puts on her shoes, and continues along her journey. She thinks to herself, "If I keep trying, I can do anything." She is back in the forest just a bit farther upstream. Soon she hears the faint whisper of Grandma Tree.

Sabrina goes in the direction of the whisper until she reaches the huge oak tree. Sabrina moves through her leaves, gently breathing in her familiar scent. She runs her hands along her weathered trunk, pushing her fingers into the maze of bark.

Sabrina has played around Grandma Tree since she was able to walk. She always found comfort in Grandma's worn bark and earthy smell. She would sometimes fall asleep in the nook of her branches. Grandma Tree is so large, and Sabrina knows that she wouldn't be able to put her arms all the way around her trunk, but Sabrina always tries.

"Hello, my child. It is great to see you!" says Grandma Tree.

"Hello, Granny. I am afraid I have lost my way. Could you please help me?"

"You have to learn to walk tall like me and be strong. Stay connected to the ground but move freely with the breeze."

Sabrina takes this wisdom to heart and thanks Grandma Tree. The dark keeps closing in on her like a big, dark blanket. But Sabrina is determined to find her way home. She inhales deeply, stands up straight and tall, and listens to her instincts. She leaves in the direction her body tells her to. She moves toward the familiar trees in the distance. She is beginning to feel more confident in her travels. She visualizes her small house up ahead. She built her tiny house out of leaves, mud, and wood. Her friends helped her gather leaves and wood. They helped her paint the window frames a pretty yellow. The door was painted turquoise. She had a vegetable patch out back that was growing pumpkins, eggplants, zucchinis, and tomatoes.

Sabrina also has a cow named Bessy, who is brown and white with soft brown eyes. She has a calf named Sammy, who is the spitting image of his mom. Bessy and Sammy keep the grass in the meadow cut short, and they love spending time with Sabrina. Each morning, Sabrina milks Bessy and makes wheels of cheese and butter from her milk.

Sabrina's stomach growls, and she realizes it has been a long time since she has eaten in the clearing with her friends. She finds a soft spot of moss at the base of a birch tree and opens her picnic basket. She eats the leftovers from the picnic. Sabrina knows she is almost home. She finishes her food and begins walking through the forest once again.

Soon, Sabrina knows where she is, and she knows her home is just ahead. She begins walking faster and soon breaks through the trees to the beautiful meadow. She sees the sun beginning to peek over the mountain beyond her house. She sees Bessy and Samuel asleep in the meadow. Sabrina says a quick hello to the sun as it brings a beautiful blue sky to the morning. She says hello to her home, her trees, and flowers. As Sabrina slowly makes her way to her house, she silently says thank you to all her friends who helped her find her way home.

Sabrina goes into her cottage, starts a fire in the fireplace, toasts a few marshmallows, and enjoys them in silence. She curls up on her bed and quickly falls asleep. She doesn't care that she has twigs, leaves, and moss in her hair because her heart is full of sunshine.

3

THE DISAPPEARANCE OF MEGHAN

"Why do I have to go to this party?" Meghan whined.

Meghan pulled her head away from her mother's hands as her mother tried to tame Meghan's curls. Her mother tried her best to get Meghan's hair out of her face, but Meghan just wouldn't be still.

"Sweet pea, you have to go. Your cousin invited you to her party, and it would be rude not to go."

"But I don't like Trista. She thinks she knows everything. She doesn't even talk to anyone; she lectures us."

Meghan's mom sighed. "Come on, let's get you dressed. Trista said she wanted you to wear your blue sundress."

Meghan groaned and rolled her eyes. She stomped behind her mother into her bedroom. Meghan's mom was in Meghan's closet searching for the blue dress. She soon emerged with the sundress and handed it to Meghan.

"Here, put this on." Meghan pulled the dress over her head and smoothed it in place.

Her mom had gone back into the closet. "Mom, what are you looking for?"

"I know you had a hat that matched the sundress."

"Oh, mom, I don't need to wear a hat."

"The party is going to be outside, and you know how easily you burn. You have to wear your hat."

Meghan groaned and rolled her eyes again. She hated hats as much as she hated wearing dresses. Mom came out of the closet and plopped the hat on top of Meghan's head. She stood back.

"There, you look so pretty."

Meghan scrunched up her face at her mom. Mom smiled at Meghan.

"I promise that you will have a wonderful time when you get there. You know how to get to your cousin's house. Just follow the path through the park. It will be a wonderful party. Aunt Hattie told me they lined the path with ribbons to help guide their guests. You can ride your bike if you would like to. Just follow the ribbons there. Don't veer off the path, and make sure you don't lose the invitation." Meghan's mom pressed the envelope into her hand.

Meghan kissed her mom and waved goodbye as she went around the back of the house to get her bike out of the garage. Meghan's bike was her favorite possession. It was a bright red that had a white basket on the handlebars. She started pushing her bike toward the path. Her black and white cat saw Meghan leaving and began following her.

"No, Oreo, you can't go." Meghan tried to shoo the cat back toward the house.

Oreo protested loudly with a meow. "Fine, come along. With you there, I might be able to tolerate the party." Meghan reached down and picked up Oreo and put him in the basket. She started off down the path.

Meghan had always loved the park. It was huge and open. All the trees were tall, and she always thought that today she would climb one. Maybe she could reach a cloud if she climbed high enough.

She soon began seeing ribbons that were tied in bows that should lead her to the party. She followed the ribbons farther into the park. Meghan groaned to herself. All she wanted was to run away and skip Trista's party.

Something to Meghan's left caught her eye. She moved her head in that direction. Just ahead of her, the path forked. Meghan had ridden and walked this path before and knew that there hadn't ever been a fork on this path, but right there in front of her, she saw the path split in two different directions. One path was smaller, and it led deeper into the forest. Meghan was a very curious girl, and she saw this path was lined with purple ribbons. Purple was her favorite color, after all. Meghan sat there a few minutes, and it almost felt like she was being pulled in two different directions. She looked at Oreo.

"That's very odd, Oreo, look. There is a brand new path. I have gone this way many times, and I know there hasn't ever been another path. Well, I have to follow it, just to see where it goes. When a person is given a chance to be surprised, you have to take it."

Oreo agreed with a meow, and off they went, following the purple ribbons. The farther they traveled down this new path, the trees started looking a lot different. The trees went from the pines she was used to seeing to a twisted type that Meghan hadn't ever seen. The color of the sky changed from a bright blue to a brilliant purple. Meghan began shivering because it had gotten cold. To Meghan's surprise, it began snowing.

"I am not dressed for this weather. It is very strange to be snowing in the middle of June."

Suddenly the path that was lined with purple ribbons stopped. Right in front of Meghan was the biggest tree she had ever seen. It was bigger than any house Meghan had seen. She began rubbing her eyes.

"Wait a minute... this tree is a house." Meghan thought.

She saw a yellow door with a gold knob that was just her size. Meghan reached out to knock on the door when the door suddenly opened by itself. Oreo began meowing and jumped out of the basket.

"Wait, Oreo, come back!" Meghan cried, but Oreo had already disappeared around the door. Meghan tossed her bike down and ran after Oreo.

Meghan slowly peeked inside. To her surprise, the tree wasn't a house. The door that opened showed a tunnel that went a lot farther than Meghan's eyes were able to see. There was a spiral stair case on the side of the tunnel that led down. Meghan leaned over the stairs. They were so deep she couldn't see the bottom, but she could hear cheerful music coming from the tunnel. Delicious scents enticed her nose.

"I can't show up at Trista's without Oreo. I have to find him."

Meghan mustered all her courage, which didn't feel like a whole lot, but a small amount is a lot more powerful than being scared.

Meghan decided to go down the stairs. She felt like she had been going downstairs for hours, but finally, she saw the bottom. She saw all kinds of animals playing instruments and dancing around a fire. There were tables, and chairs piled high with all kinds of food. It looked like all the animals were having their own party. Meghan saw birds, rabbits, wolves, foxes, badgers, and bears, all dressed in their finest, walking on their hind feet.

Meghan gasped.

This caused the music to stop as the animals turned to look at her. "Why is there a human amongst us?" asked the rabbit who was holding a guitar and dressed in green pants.

Meghan cleared her throat. "My name is Meghan, and I was trying to find my cat."

"Oh, you're talking about Mr. Oreo. He is talking to Badger." Said a bear who was in a fancy evening gown. Meghan gasped again when she saw her cat actually talking to a badger and walking on his hind legs.

"Oh, I have to be dreaming. There is no way this is happening." Meghan rubbed her eyes.

A grey fox in a tweed jacket and top hat walked up to Meghan. There was a pair of glasses sitting low on his large snout. "I'm sorry, dear, this is a private party. Do you have an invitation?"

"Um..." Meghan stuttered. She felt hungry and cold, and she wasn't about to leave her cat. She reached into her pocket where she had put Trista's invitation. She handed it to the fox.

"Oh, my, is there anyone here who can read human writing," asked the fox.

None of the animals could read it, so Meghan got a wonderful idea. She raised her hand. "I can read it. It says you are cordially invited to a party, and you may bring one guest. Oreo is my guest."

The fox looked at the invitation and said, "Alright, let us continue our party, and please find something a bit more proper for Mr. Oreo to wear. It is not decent for a feline to parade around in just their fur."

Meghan put her hat onto Oreo's head and tied a ribbon around his neck. They then sat down at one of the tables to eat. Oreo leaned over to whisper in Meghan's ear.

"That was some quick thinking. I just wanted the food. I don't know anybody here."

Meghan was still in shock, being able to understand her cat talking. They ate their fill of all the delicious food. They drank honey and milk from tiny tea cups. When the music began, Meghan danced with all the animals at the party. The rabbit even taught her a new dance. It wasn't until close to the morning that Meghan even thought about the time.

"Oh, no, I forgot about my cousin's party. I have to go. Thank you all for the wonderful time. This was the best party I have been to in my entire life." All the animals gave her a hug. "There is just one thing I don't understand. There wasn't another path anytime I have gone through the park, but today there was one?"

"Well, maybe you weren't looking for another path the other times," said the fox as he winked. "Please come back to the next party we have."

"I will. Thanks again."

Meghan and Oreo started the long climb back up the spiral staircase. They finally reached the top and went back through the red door into the park. Meghan looked around and saw Oreo was walking on all fours and had discarded his hat and ribbon. Oreo meowed and licked his paws. Meghan picked up the hat, ribbon, and Oreo and put them into her basket.

The forest began looking normal again, and the sun was still high in the sky. It was like time had just stood still. Meghan began pedaling her bike back toward where the path split. As she got closer to the fork in the road, Meghan began feeling more and more like herself. As she took the path back toward her house, she felt completely whole again. Meghan saw her house at the end of the path. Meghan hugged Oreo. "This was a wonderful day."

Meghan had a strange feeling deep inside her as memories of sitting around a table flooded her mind. She saw herself sitting there eating cucumber sandwiches and drinking weak tea, listening to her cousin Trista talk endlessly about her newest dress and hat that her mother bought her for the party. The other part of Meghan's memories took over and pushed the boring memory away. When she arrived home, she put her bike away. She bounced into her house and hugged her mother.

"Hey, did you have a good time?"

Meghan smiled to herself. "Yes, mother, I did. I had a wonderful time at the party."

"See, I told you if you just gave Trista a chance, you would have a good time."

"Yeah, I guess I just had to look at it from a different perspective."

Oreo came into the house and slinked against Meghan's legs. Meghan reached down and picked him up. He purred loudly and rubbed his face against hers.

"When did you and Oreo become friends?"

"Oh, I think we have always been friends; we just didn't know how to tell each other."

Meghan kissed Oreo on top of the head and put him down. He went scurrying away and found a ball to play with. Meghan smiled a secret smile and went to her room to change her clothes.

4

THE CASE OF THE MISSING BACKPACK

"You know there isn't a competition to see how much stuff you can put into your backpack." Mom said while shaking her head.

"But all this stuff is important...." Freddie had a weird relationship with his backpack.

It wasn't anything spectacular. It was blue and small, but Freddie had a knack for putting a lot of things into it. Freddie's backpack had many pockets and zippers that made it easier to put things into it.

That was Freddie's problem. He always said, "You never know what you might need when you are in the park or visiting friends."

"What kinds of things?" asked mom?

"Just the kinds of things that might be useful," Freddie said, smiling at the cars hanging from the zipper of the backpack. Freddie began counting things. "Balls to juggle, ropes to skip, a beach ball we can blow up, you know, just in case."

Mom knew she shouldn't ask, but she couldn't help herself, "Just in case of what?"

"Just in case someone says, has anyone got a beach ball? Then I have paper, pencils, and crayons if someone wants to draw. A puzzle or two, dice, and some games, just in case."

Freddie's mom didn't take the time to ask, but Freddie kept listing all his things.

"Bubbles, you never know when you will need to blow some bubbles just to cheer someone up. Ice cream, wait, that's silly. What I meant to say was money for ice cream in this little pocket. Jelly beans, cookies, and candies in this pocket here because that's what pockets are for."

Freddie kept on talking. "In the winter, I have some extra scarves and gloves. For summer, there is a towel, clean socks, and hat."

Mom threw her hands in the air, "I can't believe this; there is no way you need all that stuff."

Freddie didn't hesitate. "I have some books and music, you know, just in case. There is also a whistle and tambourine. And just in case, I have a few bandages and my name and address on the inside."

Mom stopped asking. She just got ready and took Freddie to the park. Later that day, she got to see "just in case" actually happen. There were actually many "just in cases."

Freddie had just taken out the skipping rope and balls for juggling and was having fun playing in the sand with his friends.

One child said, "I bet you don't have a decent ball."

Freddie laughed, "Only if you help me blow it up; I have a beach ball in here." Freddie reached into his backpack, and his mom just shook her head.

All the children shouted "hooray," and catching the beach ball was the next game. It wasn't long before a small girl fell off a swing. Freddie ran over with his backpack and covered the scratches with some bandages. He then blew some bubbles to make the little girl smile again.

Freddie shrugged at his mom, "just in case." He then handed the little girl a cookie.

When all the children got tired, they sat down in the shade. Freddie pulled out the paper and crayons, and they started the game of "Boy, Girl, Animal, and Fruit." This was their favorite word game. Freddie had just written down Bobby, Berta, Bat, and Blueberry and was moving on the F when they heard the ice cream man coming.

Freddie was reaching for his "just in case" money for ice cream, but mom gave him some instead. Once everyone had eaten their ice cream, Freddie wanted to put away the paper and crayons. He opened his mouth and cried out. "It's gone; my backpack is gone!"

Everyone around helped Freddie look for his backpack. They looked everywhere they could think of in the trees, under the swings, in the sand, in the bushes, everywhere.

His mom tried to help, "I'll buy you a new one."

"But my cars are gone, along with all the other "just in case" treasures I had in there."

Freddie began crying, and no one knew what to say to comfort him. Freddie's backpack was gone, but the worst part was his cars were gone too.

Mom finally got Freddie to leave the park. Freddie was extremely sad the rest of the day. When nighttime rolled around, mom reminded Freddie, "You put your name and address inside the backpack, didn't you... just in case?"

Freddie nodded, "Yes, just in case it got lost."

"Well, let's hope someone sees your name and address inside and brings it back to you." Mom gave Freddie a huge hug.

A couple of days passed, and mom and Freddie were coming back home from searching the park for the hundredth time. Freddie was walking slowly behind mom scuffling his feet in the dirt. Mom saw the backpack sitting by the door before Freddie.

"Hey, Freddie, can you go inside by yourself? I need to ask Mrs. Thomas something right quick?"

Freddie shrugged, "Yes, mom, I'll be fine."

Mom quickly moved into their neighbor's yard and watched Freddie from behind the rose bush. Freddie still hadn't looked up. As he got closer to the door, something blue caught his eye. Freddie looked up and couldn't believe his eyes. There sat his backpack against the door.

Freddie picked up his backpack and shouted with glee. "Mom, mom, come quickly; my backpack is back!"

Mom came quickly down the driveway. Freddie ran to greet his mom, waving the backpack in front of him.

"Look, mom, it's back! You were right; someone did bring it back."

Mom ruffled Freddie's hair, "I'm so glad. Now let's go inside and get washed up for dinner."

Freddie carried his backpack to the kitchen table and opened it up. There were a lot of things missing like the pennies for ice cream, some books, games, drinks, an orange, jelly beans, cookies, and candies.

So, now Freddie had another mystery. Who would have taken the backpack plus all the food, games, and money? The cars know, but they aren't talking.

Freddie carried his backpack into the kitchen and put it on the table. Mom looked up. "What's wrong, Freddie?"

"I just can't understand why someone would want my backpack?"

"Well, why wouldn't they. Look at all the stuff that was in it. It was full of all kinds of goodies."

"That's true. I guess you were right; I didn't need all those things."

"Well, some of those things did come in handy the other day. Don't forget that. So have you gone through the entire backpack? Have you checked every pocket and zipper?"

"Yes, I think so."

Freddie started checking every pocket and opening all the zippers. He reached his hand into one zipper, and his fingers felt a piece of paper. He wrapped his hand around the paper and pulled it out.

"Look, mom, I found this."

Freddie handed the paper to his mom. She opened it and read it. She handed it back to Freddie. "Here, read this."

The note read: "Dear little boy, I'm sorry I took your backpack. You just had so much interesting stuff in it that I had to look through it. I didn't have time to look through everything before you finished your ice cream, so I just hid it in my sister's stroller. I'm sorry I caused you so much sorrow. I know there are things missing, but I will try to replace them a little bit at a time. Please forgive me for being a thief, and I hope one day we might be friends. I will show you who I am the next time we are at the park together."

It was simply signed with a T.

These days Freddie doesn't put as many things in his backpack because he worries he might lose it again. He keeps a close watch on it when he's at the park. Freddie is a lot more careful and only puts about half of what he used to in it. He has a hard time choosing what goes into his backpack with each outing.

This time he decided not to put his whistle or tambourine in the backpack. "Nobody ever wants to blow a whistle or play with a tambourine anyway."

Every time Freddie went to the park, he always wondered if the mysterious T would show themselves to him on that day. He hoped one day they would. He wasn't mad at them. He would like to show them how they could make their own "just in case" backpack.

5

WHY DID DAD TURN INTO A MONSTER?

It was another ordinary day on the afternoon when Dad turned into a monster.

"Hey, girls, how was school today?" asked Dad.

The girls didn't reply. They just dropped their backpacks on the floor. They took off their socks and shoes and left them in a pile in the middle of the living room. It was hot, and it felt good on their feet to put them against the cool tile. Aubree flopped down into a beanbag chair in the living room. She clicked on the television.

Meredith flopped down on her stomach on the floor beside Aubree. Dad could hear them arguing about what they were going to watch.

"We watched *Pretzel and the Puppies* yesterday; I want to watch *Supernatural Academy* today," Meredith whined.

"I don't care. I'm the oldest, so I get to decide."

"Who says?"

"I do."

"Girls, you need to quit arguing and start your homework," Dad called from the kitchen.

"We always watch one show, then start our homework."

"Then put it on a show and get to it."

The arguing finally stopped, and dad heard the distinct sounds of *Alice's Wonderland Bakery*. Dad was chopping vegetables to make soup for dinner when Aubree's shrill voice broke through his silence.

"Hey, dad, bring me some cookies and milk!" shouted Aubree.

"I'd like some, too," said Meredith. She was lying on her stomach watching television.

Dad didn't reply back immediately. He actually gripped the knife in his hand a bit tighter. He felt an animal instinct welling up inside him.

Was there a time when what happened might not have happened? When his spirit may have battled to get out of its human form? Meredith or Aubree couldn't say either way.

What they do agree on is that they heard a tiny growl. They both thought it was their dog, Milo, until they realized that the dog was still in the backyard. But this moment passed, and dad was fine. Dad walked to the door of the living room.

"Did you wash your hands, girls?" Dad asked.

"Sorry, we forgot," said Aubree.

Well, they did have a billion things that were a lot more important than washing their hands when they came home from school, like dolls, books, clothes, etc. They slowly got up to wash their hands but couldn't pull their eyes off of the television screen. They stopped at the door of the living room to keep watching their show.

"Make sure you turn off the television before you leave the living room. Milk and cookies are already on the table." Dad called.

The girls groaned, turned off the television, and made their way to the kitchen. Once their hands were in the running water, they started playing instead and began splashing water everywhere. They knew it wasn't a big deal because dad was already standing there holding a towel. He would clean up the mess. It was crazy how dad always seemed to know when Aubree and Meredith were going to splash water, drop food on the floor, or something.

But on this day, something strange happened.

"Meredith!" whispered Aubree.

"What's wrong?" asked Meredith. Meredith followed Aubree's eyes. Aubree was looking up at dad.

Dad was still standing there smiling and holding the towel in his hand. But his smile seemed a bit strained and tight. There was something threatening about the way he was holding the towel, getting ready to wipe up the water.

Aubree looked like she had seen something dark in dad's eyes, in the way he smiled, as if he had a war raging inside him. It was almost like a beast was lying in wait.

Then all of a sudden, dad was himself once again. It was a bit scary for the girls. Dad looked down at his girls.

"Aubree, my sweetness, is there something wrong?"

"Um, no, I didn't say anything," mumbled Aubree.

"Your milk and cookies are waiting on you."

Aubree and Meredith quickly dried their hands and went to the table. The girls ate in silence. Dad was fine while they were eating. Meredith decided to pour milk on her cookie rather than dipping it into her milk. This caused the milk to spill on the table and into the floor. Something inside, dad twitched. He started turning a weird shade of blue. The girls ate their cookies and drank their milk faster. They dropped crumbs on the table and spilled milk everywhere.

Aubree leaned over to Meredith and whispered, "Let's go!"

They jumped up from the table but left their cups and plates where they were. They left the kitchen in a hurry, but they didn't think to pick up their shoes, socks, or backpacks. Once they were safely in Aubree's room, they heard a huge...

ROAR!!!!

Oh, no. It sounded like a beast running rampant in the kitchen. They heard pans being banged together, dishes being put in the dishwasher hurriedly, doors being banged shut, things being slammed onto the counter, and books being thrown to the floor.

"What are we going to do? We can't go outside alone, and if we try to get to the telephone, that monster will see us?"

"I don't know? We need to go see what's going on?"

Aubree and Meredith slowly emerged out of Aubree's bedroom and peeked into the kitchen. They saw a monster wearing remnants of their dad's clothes. If it was indeed their dad, he had grown huge teeth and feet. His body had swollen up to four times his normal size. He had grown hair everywhere and was pulling some out by the roots. They watched him walk down the hall toward the bathroom. He left clumps of hair as he walked. They followed these clumps of hair to the bathroom. They watched him angrily turn on the faucet and watched as he violently scrubbed the vanity, mirror, toilet, and bathtub.

He took the dirty towels out of the hamper, picked up the towels and washcloths Aubree and Meredith had left lying on the floor, and left the bathroom. The girls quickly hid in the doorway of Aubree's room so their dad/monster wouldn't see them. He walked to the laundry room and shoved the dirty towels into the washing machine, and slammed the door shut. He poured detergent into the machine and started it. They heard him growl as he went past Aubree's room and back to the kitchen.

They were terrified.

"What happened to dad?" Meredith asked. "He has turned into a monster! He is on a cleaning rampage. What has he done to our real dad?"

Meredith looked around Aubree's room. They didn't have any weapons. They just had books, blocks, and toys. Aubree grabbed a big book and a pencil. Meredith grabbed a pillow.

They slowly opened the door just a bit and carefully looked out. They slowly started down the hallway toward the kitchen. They could hear dad/monster rattling around in there again. They weren't watching where they were going, so when they turned the corner in the living room, they ran right into their mom. Mom looked at her girls and saw the fear in their eyes. She stopped smiling.

"What's going on? What are you two doing?"

"Dad has turned into a monster!" Aubree exclaimed.

"Oh, I see. So you think a book, pencil, and pillow are going to help?"

The girls shrugged. "We don't know. We've never fought a dad/monster before."

Mom smiled down at her scared little girls. "You can't fight a dad/monster with a book, pencil, and pillow. Sit down, and I'll tell you what you need to do."

Mom proceeded to tell them what they would need to fight a monster. They didn't believe her but proceeded to do what she told them.

They started in the kitchen, where they picked up their shoes, socks, and backpacks. They put their dirty socks in the laundry hamper, put their shoes in their closet, and put their backpacks on the desk in their rooms. Meredith and Aubree noticed that with every chore they did, dad's size decreased just a bit.

Aubree went to a drawer in the kitchen and got out some dishrags and towels. She wiped up all the water they left on the sink and floor. She handed a cloth to Meredith, who wiped off the kitchen table. Aubree brought the towel over and cleaned up the spilled milk off the floor. Once the girls were through cleaning the kitchen, dad had stopped gnashing his teeth.

They finished cleaning up their mess and slowly walked toward their dad. They hugged him, and miraculously he turned back into their loving dad. It was a very magical moment.

From that day on, Meredith and Aubree never forgot the way to tame a monster if they happened to create one.

They had to remember that because one day when they got out of the pool, mom had turned into a monster.

6

THE SAFE

Paul was an extremely wealthy man. He has many employees working for him. Paul loved his house, and he treated his employees very well. He also loved his job. He didn't have to work, but he enjoyed what he did. He was the most ruthless defense attorney in town. If you are in need of a good defense attorney if you can find him, and if you can afford him, I promise you, he will help you. He hadn't lost a case in over 20 years.

Paul did have one flaw, and that is he kept a huge amount of money locked in a safe in his bedroom. He did this so he had money on hand anytime he needed it. Paul checked his money every morning and night. He knew exactly how much money was in his safe to the last dollar.

Paul had been working on a grueling murder case that was wearing him down. He was sure his client was innocent but couldn't find that one piece of evidence to prove his innocence. He knew he would find it, but time was running out, and he just couldn't figure out what he was overlooking.

Paul came home that same day, ate his dinner, and went to the library in his house to relax. He sat in his favorite chair and picked up the book he had been reading for some time. Liza, one of his employees, came into the library and poured him a glass of brandy. She set the snifter on a coaster along with a basket of cookies that had just come out of the oven.

Paul's nose sniffed the air. "Fresh baked cookies, yum. Thank you, Liza."

Liza bowed slightly. "You are welcome, Mr. Paul."

"We wouldn't have any coffee brewed in the kitchen, would we?"

"I do believe Pearl just put on a pot. Would you like me to bring you a cup?"

"Yes, please, with a splash of cream and two spoons of sugar."

"Right away, sir."

Liza left and returned to the kitchen. She poured a cup of coffee for Paul and quickly added the sugar and cream. She gave it a quick stir and carefully carried it back to the library. Liza noticed one of the newer employees hanging around upstairs near Mr. Paul's bedroom. This particular employee was hired to take care of Paul's car. He was supposed to check all the fluids in Paul's car daily and change whatever needed to be changed.

Liza remembered what she was supposed to be doing when the coffee in the cup sloshed out and burned her finger. She sucked in a breath and carried the cup into the library. She sat it down on a coaster and apologized to Paul for taking so long. Paul looked up from his book and thanked her.

Liza bowed once again. "If there is nothing else, I am going home now."

"Sure, Liza, I'm sorry to have kept you so long."

"Oh, no problem, sir."

"Have a good evening, Liza."

"You, too, sir."

Liza hesitated a moment, wondering if she should say something to Paul about Henry. She decided not to as she wanted to get home to her daughter so they could watch their favorite show together.

Paul ate the cookies and drank his coffee and brandy while he read two more chapters in his book. His eyes began burning, and the words on the page began running together. He marked his place in the book, took his dirty dishes to the kitchen, and made his way upstairs to his room. He went into his bathroom and took his evening shower. He put on his pajamas and walked back out into his room. There was an unfamiliar scent in his room, but he couldn't place it. He thought that it might be some of the flowers that had been brought into his room. Paul went over to his safe, put in the password, and opened it. He counted all the money, closed the safe, and went to sleep.

A few days passed, and Paul was still worried about the murder case he was working on. He went about his normal routine with the case still rolling around in his mind. He went to his room, took a hot shower to try and relax, and decided to go ahead and check his safe. Paul put in the password and opened his safe to find it completely empty. Paul immediately called his private investigator, Blake.

Paul began crawling around on the floor, looking for clues. Paul noticed that same smell he had smelled a few nights before. It wasn't long before Blake arrived, and they both started looking for clues. Blake found some weird fibers under Paul's bed. He showed them to Paul. Blake and Paul both sniffed them.

"That's the scent I smelled the other night. Whoever these fibers came off of is the one who stole my money. What I can't understand is how they got my password to the safe."

"Maybe they snuck in here, laid under your bed so they could see you open the safe, waited for you to go to sleep, and then snuck back out. They waited until today while you were at work, snuck back in here, put in your password, and took your money."

"That is exactly what I was thinking, too, Blake. But how am I going to find them?"

"You could line up all your employees and just sniff them."

Paul smiled and said, "If I have to, but I think I can get them to show themselves before then."

Paul called all his employees into the great room. "I know everyone wants to go home, but the money in my safe has been taken."

Paul paused as gasps went up around the room.

"Blake has found some evidence under my bed that will soon lead us to the thief. This evidence has a very distinct smell if everyone will just stand still while we mingle through the room and give everyone a quick sniff."

Paul and Blake noticed the employees begin sniffing themselves. Paul noticed George moving closer and closer to the door as he talked. Paul nudged Blake and rolled his eyes in the direction of George.

"George, do you need to leave?" Paul asked.

George didn't hesitate; he began running toward the door. A few of the other employees grabbed him and brought him back into the room.

"George, did you take my money?"

George hung his head, "Yes, sir, I did."

"Why? Do I not pay you enough?"

"Yes, you pay me enough. I just got into debt with some bad men. I have a gambling problem, and I owe them a lot of money."

"Okay, how much do you owe them?"

George looked around at his fellow employees. He leaned closer to Paul, "$5,000."

"Is that all?"

"Is that all? That's a lot of money for someone like me."

"I would have given you the money if you had just asked."

"I was too embarrassed."

"Too embarrassed to ask for money, but you will steal it from me?"

"I know I've messed up bad. I'll go get your money and then leave. I will find a job some place else."

"Why would you need to look for a different job? Did I fire you?"

George looked at Paul in disbelief. "You aren't going to fire me for stealing from you?"

"No, I'm going to give you the money you need to pay off these men, and you are going to help me get these men arrested."

"Yes, sir, I will do whatever you ask of me."

Together, Paul, Blake, and George created a plan to trap the bookies. These men had many outstanding warrants for illegal gambling, murder, kidnapping, and many other offenses. During the time they were working on the plan to get these men arrested, it dawned on Paul how the murder was done to prove his client's innocence.

The next day, Blake went with George to pay off his debt and to make sure nothing went wrong with their plan so they could get these men behind bars. Paul went to court to prove his client's innocence.

Paul demonstrated how his client couldn't have committed the murder because of the angle of the shot. If his client had shot the victim, the trajectory of the bullet would have gone into the victim at a 45-degree angle from above, but the trajectory of the bullet was at a 45-degree angle from below. This meant that someone had been lying under the victim's bed and shot them. They then planted the gun in Paul's client's gym bag to frame them. Paul's client would have been too tall to fit under the victim's bed, but there was one person in the courtroom that would have been a perfect fit. When this person stood up to leave the courtroom, the judge asked the bailiffs to detain them. The prosecutor dropped the charges against Paul's client.

The prosecutor was extremely busy for a couple of weeks as she had six men she was creating cases against, and she was determined not to lose any of them. Paul agreed not to defend any of them to give her a chance at winning, plus Paul wanted these people behind bars for the greater good of the town.

7

THE CASE OF THE MISSING BALL

Mark and Charlotte are siblings. They are good children and haven't caused their parents any trouble. They love helping their family and friends find lost things. When they are looking for lost things, they always pretend they are the world's best detectives. They each have a magnifying glass and a telescope. They use the telescope to see things that are far away.

Both Charlotte and Mark love playing sports, especially soccer. They would spend hours at the park kicking and throwing their soccer ball at each other. Every now and then, some of the other children would ask to join their game, and soon, they would have lots of friends playing a game of soccer. When one of these games started, it usually went on until it started getting dark, and the children, one by one, would tell Mark and Charlotte goodbye and thanks for the game. Eventually, Mark and Charlotte would stop playing and go back to their home, too.

On this particular day, Mark and Charlotte opened the door to be greeted by their dog, Tiny. Now, Tiny was an English bulldog. He had the most adorable smushed-up nose and wrinkled face. One thing about Tiny is even though he was extremely cute, he was just as naughty, but everyone who saw Tiny fell in love with him. He was a lovable dog and loved everyone in return. Tiny was all the time getting into things that he shouldn't be getting into. He would steal socks, shoes, toys, basically anything he could get in his mouth. Tiny never chewed on anything he stole; he just hid them. Socks had been found under the rose bushes in the backyard. Mom found her favorite pair of heels in the garage under dad's workbench. Dad found some missing tools under Mark's bed. Charlotte found her favorite stuffed animal in the pantry. No one could stay mad at Tiny. Just one look at his cute, little, smushed-up face, and people's hearts would melt. He had the saddest brown eyes that made you just want to kiss his head rather than scold him. Tiny loved to play with Mark and Charlotte's soccer ball just as much as they did.

Tiny was bouncing around Mark and Charlotte's feet as they tried to get in the house. He jumped up and knocked the soccer ball out of Mark's arms with his nose.

"Okay, okay, we'll go outside and play some soccer with you, but we've got to get washed up for dinner."

Mark and Charlotte ran out the back door and into the yard with Tiny right on their heels. Both kids were laughing, and Tiny was bouncing and running all over the yard chasing the ball. Tiny would hit the ball with his nose and then bark while running after it. Mark and Charlotte would try to play keep-away with Tiny, but he could jump higher than most bulldogs. He would jump and hit the ball, making it go in another direction, then he would bark and chase after it. The three played until mom stuck her head out the back door and yelled for them to come to eat.

Mark scooped up the ball and carried it back into the house. He put it on his favorite chair in the family room and went to wash his hands for dinner. Charlotte followed Mark into the bathroom they shared and washed her hands, too. Both children walked into the dining room and took their place at the table. They ate while telling their parents about their day at the park and all the fun they had playing soccer with the other kids in the neighborhood.

Charlotte helped mom clear the table and did the dishes, and then she went to take a bath. Once she was through with her bath, she kissed her parents good night and went to her room to read before bed.

Dad had asked Mark for some help taking out the trash and putting the recyclables into the bin for pick up the next day. By the time they were through, Mark was ready for his bath. He took his bath, kissed his parents good night, peeked into Charlotte's room and told her a quick good night, and went off to his room. He didn't even think about the soccer ball.

Mark and Charlotte's minds were on school more than soccer because they had to take tests to see if they could move on to the next grade in school. All the free time they had, they spent studying. Mark was ready to move to middle school, but Charlotte was going to miss her brother being at the same school. Charlotte had other friends, but her best friend would always be her brother.

The week of tests was done, and Mark had been thinking about relaxing while kicking the soccer ball around all day. On the way home from school, he mentioned this to Charlotte.

"Hey, do you feel like playing some soccer when we get home?"

Charlotte's eyes lit up, "Sure, that sounds great."

They walked home as quickly as they could. They opened the door to find Tiny waiting on them. They bent down and gave him some quick scratches on his head. They carried their backpacks to their room, changed their clothes, and went to the kitchen for a quick snack. Mom had put some cookies and milk on the kitchen table along with some apples, peanut butter, and cheese. They ate quickly as they were excited to have the tests over and to get to play with their soccer ball.

Mark was the first one to get through eating, and he took his dishes to the sink and rinsed them before he put them in the dishwasher. He then ran to his room to get the soccer ball out of his closet. When Mark opened his closet door, he didn't see his soccer ball. He went back into the kitchen just as Charlotte was putting her dishes in the dishwasher.

"Charlotte, have you seen the soccer ball?"

"No, isn't it in your closet?"

"No, I just checked."

Mark went to the living room and asked mom. "Mom, have you seen our soccer ball?"

"No, honey, I'm sorry I haven't. When was the last time you remember having the ball?"

Mark thought for a few minutes. "The last time I remember playing with it was last week when we played outside with Tiny. I remember you yelled for us to come in and eat dinner. I brought the ball in and put it on my chair. I ate, helped dad with the trash, took my bath, and went to bed."

Mark went into the family room, but the ball wasn't in his chair. By this time, Charlotte was following Mark around.

"Where could the ball be?"

"I don't know, but we have an official mystery on our hands."

"Cool. I'm going to get my magnifying glass."

"Cool. I'll get mine, too. We'll see if we can come up with some clues."

Mark and Charlotte grabbed their detective gear and met back in the family room. Charlotte had her notebook out, ready to take notes about the clues they found. Mark was using his magnifying glass and was looking at his chair from every angle. He crawled around on the floor under the chair.

"Ah, ha!" Mark exclaimed.

"Did you find something?"

"Yes, it's our first clue."

"What is it?"

Mark had picked up something with the tweezers from his detective kit. He showed it to Charlotte. Her eyes grew large and excited. They knew Tiny loved stealing and hiding things, but it was normally small things that he could easily put into his mouth. He couldn't pick up the soccer ball without popping it.

"Okay, so we know Tiny probably took the ball, but how and where did he hide it?" Charlotte asked.

"That's the new mystery."

They went back to the living room to talk to their mom.

"Mom, have you noticed Tiny spending more time in one place than anywhere else?"

"Not really. Do you think he took your ball?"

"Yeah, we found this at my chair."

Mark showed mom the hair that he found on his chair.

"Well, if Tiny took the ball, wouldn't he have popped it?"

"We aren't sure. We hope not, but we won't know until we find it."

"Well, let's go see if we can find Tiny."

Mark, Charlotte, and Mom began looking around the house to see if they could find Tiny. All of them heard the little snorting noise he makes when he's happy and playing with a toy. They followed the sound, and it led them out into the backyard. They could see Tiny's rump sticking out from behind his dog house. His little nubby of a tail was wagging as hard as it could wag. Mark, Charlotte, and Mom peeked in behind and over Tiny's dog house. There was Tiny booping the ball with his nose. The ball would hit the side of the garage and then bounce back and hit his nose. He was having the best time playing with the soccer ball all by himself.

"Oh, Tiny, you took the ball," Mark exclaimed. "We're sorry we haven't had a lot of time to play with you this week."

"But we can play now if you want to," Charlotte said.

Tiny gave a bark and hit the ball with his nose harder to bounce it out into the yard. The three friends played with the soccer ball until dinner time. This time when mom called them for dinner, Mark scooped the ball up and put it in his closet before he washed his hands.

After dinner, Mark found Tiny sitting in front of his closet door whining. He patted Tiny's head. "We'll play tomorrow. I promise."

8

HOW DID THE CAR GET INSIDE THE MALL

Will Cole was a security guard at the local mall. He loved his job and did the job the best he could. His favorite part of the day was patrolling the mall while it was still closed. He would check every nook and cranny to make sure no one was there who wasn't supposed to be there.

On this particular day, Will was walking through the mezzanine. He loved this part of the mall. It had lots of floor-to-ceiling windows, skylights, and a big open area. It was always bright and sunny, and at night you could see the stars. Will was making his way across the mezzanine to the stairs that take you to the second floor. He noticed something strange in the middle of the mezzanine. As he got closer, he realized it was a car.

It wasn't just any car; it was a 1970 Chevrolet Chevelle. It was the most beautiful shade of blue Will had ever seen on a car. Will walked all the way around the car. He opened the doors, popped the hood, and even crawled under the car. Everything was intact. There wasn't anything that had been left off. All the badging had even been put onto the car.

"How in the world did a car get inside the mall." Will wondered.

Will began looking around. He thought surely that some of his other guards were pranking him. He kept looking around, waiting on the other guards to jump out and say, "surprise." He waited about 15 minutes and decided that it wasn't a prank. It was almost time to open the mall, and he hadn't finished his rounds yet. He walked around the car one more time and then headed up the stairs. He walked quickly so he could get the doors opened on time. But what was everyone going to say that saw the car? Would the car cause a big hassle in the middle of the mall?

How could Will keep all the people in the mall from gathering around the car and touching it until he figured out who it belonged to, where it came from, and how it got into the mall. He wasn't sure that this was an actual emergency, but he decided to call 9-1-1.

"Hello, what is your emergency?"

"Well, I'm not sure I have an emergency."

"Sir, do you know it is against the law to make a false 9-1-1 call that is punishable by fines and time in jail?"

"Yes, I know, but I don't know who else to call."

"Okay, so what do you need help with?"

"Well, I am a security guard at Central Mall, and as I was making my early morning walk through, I found a car in the middle of the mall."

"A car in the mall."

"Yes."

"How did a car get in the middle of the mall?"

"I don't know; that's why I'm calling you. I don't know what else to do."

"Well, sir, this is one that I have not encountered until today. I guess I could send the police over to see if they can find any clues. Can you hang on a few minutes, let me talk to my supervisor about this?"

"Sure, I'm not going anywhere."

Will kept walking around the Chevelle as the music played in his ear. He was still trying to figure out how to keep people away from the car until he could figure out who it belonged to. He jumped when the 9-1-1 operator came back on the line.

"Sir, are you still there?"

"Yes, I'm here."

"Okay, my supervisor told me to go ahead and dispatch the police. They aren't coming as an emergency, so if there is any way you could keep people away from the car until they get there, please do."

"Yeah, I can put up some caution tape around the car, and I'll stand guard so nobody touches the car...." Will's voice trailed off as he realized his fingerprints were all over the car from where he had touched it earlier.

"Sir, are you okay?"

"No, yes, um, well, we might have a problem."

"What might that be, sir?"

"Well, when I saw the car earlier, it took my breath away. It is my all-time favorite car. I opened the doors, popped the hood, and crawled under it. My fingerprints are all over the car."

"Well, that can't be helped. Just explain to the police what happened, and they will get your prints to compare them to the ones they find on the car."

"Okay, thanks. Have a good day."

"You, too."

Will hung up the phone and called his boss. "Hey, Philip, I hate to bother you this early, but we have a problem down here."

"What kind of problem?"

"A 4,000-pound problem."

"4,000 pounds? Are there elephants in the mall?"

"Nope, not elephants. I would know what to do with elephants. I'd just call the zoo."

"What are you talking about, Will?"

"There is a 1970 Chevrolet Chevelle in the middle of the mall."

"You're kidding me?"

"I wish I was."

"Okay, have you called anybody else?"

"Yeah, I called 9-1-1. They are sending the police over. I just have to keep everyone away from the car until the police get here. I'm going to place caution tape around the car and keep watch until they get here."

"Okay, I'll get there as soon as I can."

"Okay." Will hung up with his boss and went to the security office to get the caution tape out of the supply closet. By the time he got back to the car and surrounded it with tape, some of the mall workers were beginning to make their way inside. Some of them came over to the car to check it out.

"Oh, man, that's a nice car! Are we having some kind of contest, and this is the prize?"

"Oh, wow! I always wanted a car like this. Nice!"

"Oh, my first boyfriend drove a car like this!"

"Wow, my grandfather had a car like this, but his was red."

As Will was trying to field all the questions and comments about the car, two police cruisers drove up to the front door of the mall. Four officers got out of the cars and made their way into the mall. They walked over to Will.

"Hello, are you Will?"

"Yes, I am."

"You are the one who found the car?"

"Yep."

"Did you touch anything?"

Will hung his head. "Yes, I'm sorry. I couldn't help it. I opened the driver's door, popped the hood, and crawled under the car to see if everything was intact."

"That's okay. I would have probably done the same thing," said one of the officers.

Another officer asked, "Did you see anybody suspicious or who didn't belong here?"

"No."

The officers split up and began walking through the mall. They picked up, bagged, and tagged all kinds of things they found.

They found some hairs in the trunk and on the driver's door. It was too dark to have been Will's hair, so that was a point in his favor.

A crowd began forming around the car, with all kinds of questions being asked. Will and the police officers were doing their best to field their questions but just couldn't keep ahead of them.

One of the officers clicked his mic and said a few words. "We should have some back up here in a few minutes. In the meantime, are there any doors that fold open larger than others that would allow a car like this to be driven inside the mall?"

"Not that I'm aware of, but I've only been here for six months. I've explored every inch of this mall during my lunch and breaks and haven't noticed anything like that."

It wasn't long before backup arrived, and they began moving people away from the car. It was a bit chaotic for about two hours while the officers investigated everything, and they asked all the mall employees if they had noticed anyone strange or who didn't belong in or around the mall late last night before closing. Suddenly Will remembered they had security cameras set up throughout the mall. Maybe one of the cameras caught something or someone. Will walked up to one of the detectives and told them about the security cameras.

The detective looked up. "Are you serious?"

"Yes." Will pointed to all the globes hanging from the ceiling. "All of those globes up there are cameras. There are other cameras set up at specific entrances to some of the stores."

"Then let's go see what we can see."

Will lead the detective to the security office. Once they were inside the office, Will punched a code into the computer, and all the tiny screens came to life. As they sat there watching the security footage, the other officers and detectives had been going over the mall and car. They found an ID badge inside the car. The badge belonged to a man whose name was Justin Winger, and he worked for Baker's Body Shop. Two officers were on their way there now to talk to see if Justin was at work today. Two other officers were sent to Justin's house to see if he was at home.

Will and the detective watched as a man, who they later identified as Justin, brought the car into the mall in pieces. Then they watched as he put the car together piece by piece until it was in perfect working order. They even watched as he started up the car and backed it to where it was sitting right now.

The detective clicked his mic and informed all the other officers about what they had witnessed on the security cameras. When the police officers that had been sent to Baker's Body Shop heard what Justin had done, they asked him why.

"It was a bet. A friend of mine bet me $500 that I couldn't take a car completely apart, take it to the mall, and put it back together inside the mall. I knew I could do it, so I did it. I know I broke the law by breaking into the mall, but you have to admit it was awesome."

"Yes, it was awesome, but you have to get it out of the mall."

"I will as soon as my friend sees it inside the mall and pays me what he owes me. I should have it out of the mall by tomorrow."

"Thank you so much."

"Are you going to give me a ticket or something?"

"I'll talk to the mall owners and see if they want to press charges for breaking and entering, but I think if you can promise that you can have the car out of there by tomorrow, they won't press any charges."

That night Will waited for Justin to get to the mall to let him. Will sat on the stairs and watched as Justin took the car apart piece by piece and loaded it onto a trailer parked outside the doors. When the car was completely disassembled, Will walked Justin out and locked the doors behind him.

9

MARGARET'S HORRIBLE WEEK

M argaret owned a huge architecture company. She had built some of the most prestigious houses in Allentown. She had also designed some of the biggest buildings in town. She was the most popular architect around. Margaret had a business partner by the name of Nichole. They went through college together and decided to start their own business when they graduated. Nichole was a bit jealous of Margaret because Margaret was better at customer service, giving presentations, and getting clients. Margaret also had more money.

Margaret was in her office at home when she got a call. The person on the other end of the line threatened Margaret. She just laughed and figured it was a practical joke and didn't think anything more about it. She did tell her son Peter about it. He wanted to call the cops right then, but Margaret said it was nothing but a practical joke.

On Monday, Margaret jumped out of bed to get ready for the presentation she had to give to the town council to see if they would approve her permits to build a new 30-floor apartment building. She went into her bathroom and took a shower like she did every morning before work. She washed her hair and wrapped it in a towel to let it dry while she washed the rest of her body. Margaret finished her shower, shut off the water, stepped out of the tub, and proceeded to dry herself with her favorite teal fluffy towel.

Margaret went over to the sink, opened the medicine cabinet door, and took out the toothpaste; she took her purple toothbrush out of the cup and squeezed some toothpaste onto it. She dampened it with some water and proceeded to brush her teeth. When finished, she rinsed her mouth with clean water and dried her mouth on the hand towel hanging beside the sink. She quickly applied her makeup which only took a few minutes because she only wore a bit of eye shadow, blush, and powder. Her lashes were thick and long, so she only had to apply a light coat of mascara. To finish off her makeup, she applied a light pink lip gloss.

Without taking her hair out of its towel, she walked into her bedroom and took out her blue suit, a white blouse, and a pair of nude heels. She quickly dressed and went back into the bathroom to do her hair. She bent over at the waist, unwrapped the towel, and flipped her long hair over her back. She reached for her comb as she faced the mirror to comb out her hair. When she looked at her reflection in the mirror, she screamed.

Peter, her son, came running into her room. "Mom, are you okay?"

"Okay, am I okay? Look at my hair, Peter!" Margaret screamed.

Peter stared at his mom in disbelief. Her hair was the brightest shade of orange he had ever seen. "How... how did your hair turn orange?"

"I don't know, Peter; if I knew, it wouldn't have surprised me."

"What are you going to do?"

"I'm not sure. Maybe I can pull it up and hide it with a hat."

"Hey, that might work."

Margaret quickly pulled her hair up into a high bun and secured it with hair pins. She went to her closet and found a pretty off-white hat that had different colored flowers around the band. There was a blue flower that matched her suit perfectly. She turned to face Peter.

"So, how do I look?"

"Honestly, mom, you look fabulous. Nobody is going to know that you have orange hair."

"Thanks, Peter. Now, I've got to run. Wish me luck."

"You don't need luck; you are Margaret Byrd, the greatest architect this town has ever seen."

Margaret quickly kissed her son on the cheek and headed out the door. She blew the town council away with her presentation and left with all the permits she would need to get the apartment building built. She was sitting in her office when she heard a knock at her door.

"Come in."

To Margaret's surprise, her business partner and so-called friend entered her office. Nichole looked at Margaret's hat and smirked.

"Nice hat."

"Thanks, thought I'd try something different today."

"It actually looks good on you. I heard you blew the town council away with your presentation."

"Yep, should be able to break ground by the end of the week."

"Congratulations."

"Thanks again. Was there anything else you needed?"

"Nope, just wanted to come to congratulate you."

"Okay, I've got to get to work on the Miller project. I have to put the finishing touches on their presentation."

"When did you have to give that one?"

Margaret looked at her calendar and said, "Next Tuesday."

Nichole made a mental note and nodded. "Well, I'll let you get back to it then."

"Thanks. Have a good day."

"Yeah, you, too."

When Margaret got home that night, she went straight to her bathroom and checked her shampoo and conditioner. She poured them both into her sink. Sure enough, the shampoo and conditioner were both a bright orange color. She poured them down the drain and called her hairdresser. He worked her into his schedule the next morning.

Margaret's hair was back to normal, new shampoo and conditioner had been bought, and she was putting the finishing touches on the Miller's project. The next few days went by smoothly for Margaret.

The day before the Miller's presentation, it was sweltering hot outside, and Margaret had been outside most of the day walking around the grounds of the new apartment building and the Miller's house. By the time she got home, she was beyond hot. There was only one thing on her mind, and that was diving into her pool and cooling off. When she got home, she went into the pool house and changed into her swimsuit. She dove into the pool and immediately felt refreshed as the cool water closed around her body. She swam to the end of the pool and back before she climbed onto a pool float.

Margaret had dozed off a bit when she was woken by her son screaming.

"Mom, oh my god, mom. What have you done?"

Margaret shielded her eyes from the sun and looked at her son. "What are you yelling about?"

Peter had made his way around to the side of the pool closer to his mom. "Mom, look at your skin. It's blue."

"What?" Margaret squinted against the setting sun and looked at her arm. She screamed a cry of frustration. "How are these things happening to me? Who would do this to me?"

"I don't know, mom, but we do have the security cameras you installed last month. We might be able to see who did this."

"Yeah, good idea."

Margaret paddled over to the side of the pool and climbed out. She immediately went into the pool house and showered to see if she could get any of the blue dye off of her skin. Some of it did seem to come off, but she was still a pale shade of blue. With her blonde hair, she looked like Smurfette.

She changed into a pair of shorts and a tank top and went back into the house to her office. Peter was already there, pulling up the security footage. When he changed it to the one at the pool, it wasn't long before they saw a person dressed in black pushing a cart with two 55-gallon drums of some kind of liquid on it toward the pool. The person pushed the cart to the edge of the pool. They opened the top of one and pushed it into the pool. They then opened the top of the second one and pushed it into the pool. The person in black used a pool scrubber to pull the barrels over to the edge of the pool. They reached into the pool and pulled the drums out of the pool.

Unfortunately for them, they didn't think to put on a pair of gloves, and their hands were dyed blue in that short amount of time. You could see the person in black desperately trying to get the blue off of their hands. They then walked back around to the side of the house and weren't seen again.

Peter and Margaret sat there in disbelief, wondering who in their right mind would do something like this to Margaret. Whoever it was would be easy to find because their hands would be colored blue. All they had to do was be on the lookout for a person with blue hands.

Margaret gathered all her reserve and decided to dress in slacks, a short-sleeved blouse, and a blazer. The only things that would be seen would be her face and hands. With the right amount of makeup, she could hide the blue tinge on her face; she would just put a pair of gloves on her hands.

The more Margaret thought about hiding behind the dye, the more she didn't want to. She was pretty sure it was Nichole having these things done to her. She was going to show the world that she wasn't afraid. Margaret did wear the slacks, blouse, and blazer, but she didn't hide her face behind makeup, nor did she hide her hands under gloves. Margaret walked into her office with her head held high. It wasn't long before there was a crowd of people gathering outside her office. She noticed Nichole talking to a large man wearing a janitor's uniform. The cart he was pushing was very similar to the one that was carrying the drums of dye that were used in her pool. Margaret walked out of her office and toward the man. She was at him before he had time to get onto the elevator.

"Hello, Tom. I see you are wearing gloves today. Any special reason why?"

"Um... no?"

"I'm going to need to see your hands, Tom."

Tom looked from Margaret to Nichole. He knew Margaret had the clout to keep him from working again.

"I'm sorry, Nichole, I have to work. I have children to take care of." Tom turned to Margaret. "I'm sorry, Ms. Byrd. Nichole paid me a lot of money to put that dye into your pool. She was trying to sabotage your presentations. She thought if you showed up with your skin dyed blue or your hair orange, people wouldn't take you seriously."

"Did you put the orange dye into my shampoo and conditioner?"

"No, ma'am, I did not. Nichole did that. She bought the exact same products, put the dye in them, and swapped them out the night you had your dinner party. She was very upset when you outsmarted her by pulling your hair up and hiding it under a hat. Today I see you decided to show everyone that you aren't afraid of being made fun of."

"You are right, Tom. I'm not hiding behind someone's tricks. I will face the Miller's looking the way I look now and explain to them what happened. My looks don't have anything to do with the way I run my business."

"Good for you, Ms. Byrd."

Margaret turned to Nichole. "I think you better clean out your office and be gone by the time I am finished with the Miller's presentation. I don't want to hear anything about you owning part of this business. I am the one who keeps the clients we have and brings in new clients. When was the last time you brought in a new client? Can't think of one, can you? It was ten years ago when your ex-husband hired us to build his new auto shop. I even did it for way under what it should have cost. We lost money on that one, and you know it. Be gone before I call the police. With Tom's testimony, I think I have a pretty good case of breaking and entering and attempt to do bodily harm."

Nichole knew she was beaten. She hung her head, walked to her office, and had it cleaned out before lunch. Margaret explained to the Millers what had happened, and they were so impressed with her candor and strength they asked her to create some blueprints for their daughter's house they wanted to build for her as a wedding present.

10

THE CASE OF THE MISSING GIRAFFE

It was a sunny summer day when Penny was playing in the backyard with her dog, Samson. Mom and Dad were sitting on the patio at the table drinking coffee. Dad was reading the newspaper.

"Hmm... have you heard the news?"

"What news?" asked Penny and mom.

"There is a giraffe missing from the zoo."

Penny looked up from playing with Samson. "Do they know where it went?"

"Not really; one of the zookeepers found that it was missing when he opened the zoo this morning, and he was checking on the animals. They are giving a reward to the person who finds the giraffe."

"Do you think we should help find it?" asked mom.

"Of course, we need to go help find it," said Penny.

They all climbed into the car and took a ride to the zoo. Dad bought everyone a ticket, and they started walking around the zoo. They went from one animal to another, always on the lookout for a large giraffe.

"Make sure you keep your eyes peeled for clues."

As they made their way around the zoo, they stopped to look at the elephants, but they didn't see a giraffe in their pen. Their next stop was the lion's den, but they didn't see a giraffe in their den either. They moved on to the rhinoceros, and again, they didn't see a giraffe. Next to the rhinoceros was the hippopotamus. The only part of the hippos that they saw was their eye sticking out of the water. It was a hot day, and the hippos were trying to stay cool.

Penny wanted to ride the camels, so their next stop was the camel ride. Penny thought being on the back of a camel would help her see over the tops of buildings and things so she could spot the giraffe. She rode around on top of the camel but still didn't see a giraffe.

They noticed a very tall old lady dressed in a cute purple dress, with a purple scarf, purple purse, and grey hair wearing glasses. She asked them if they had heard about the missing giraffe.

Mom and Dad replied, "Yes, that's why we decided to come to the zoo."

But Penny wasn't so sure. Penny looked at the very tall old lady again. Penny had a very weird feeling about the tall lady, but they kept looking around at all the animals. They went to the monkey enclosure, and Penny made faces at all the monkeys. Some of the monkeys even made faces back at Penny.

The next pen was the bears. Penny loved bears. She stood at the edge of the enclosure and looked down at the bears.

"Be careful, Penny; we don't want you to fall in."

"Don't worry, mom; I'll be careful."

Just then, a worker came by with a cart of food for the bears. Penny walked over to the cart.

"Hey, mom, they eat vegetables just like me."

The worker looked at Penny. "Would you like to throw them some food down?"

"May I please?"

"Sure. Do you see that big box right there?" The lady pointed to a huge black box in the middle of their enclosure that was almost right below them.

"Yes."

"Try to hit that box."

Penny was amazed when the bears began walking over to where they were standing. They stopped right below Penny. Penny was so excited she was bouncing up and down.

"Mom, look, they're coming over to me. They know I'm going to feed them."

"I'm watching, sweetheart." Mom had taken her camera out and was taking pictures of Penny feeding the bears. This was a moment she had wanted to remember for a long time, and she knew Penny would want these pictures.

Penny grabbed a summer squash and threw it over the fence. It landed right in the middle of the black box. One big old bear watched as the squash came down and grabbed it up and ate it.

Penny then grabbed a large chunk of watermelon and gave it a toss. Another bear walked right under where Penny and the lady were standing. It opened its mouth, and the watermelon fell right into its mouth.

"Mom, mom, did you see that? It caught the watermelon in its mouth."

Mom and Dad were smiling like crazy. "Yes, dear, we saw."

Penny and the lady kept throwing the fruits and vegetables down to the bears until the cart was empty. The lady thanked Penny for her help, and she left to go feed another animal. Penny stood for a long time, just watching the bears munch on their food. When the bears finally got their bellies full and began wandering off to find some shade for a nap, Penny moved from her spot.

Penny skipped ahead of her mom and dad, happy as could be. She led them down a path that went into a wooded area toward the moose. It wasn't long before Penny began hearing the moose crunching around in the forest, stepping on twigs, sticks, and leaves. Penny stopped for a moment but didn't see any signs of a giraffe.

As they came back out of the forest, the next enclosure was the kangaroos. Penny stopped for a moment to watch a joey climb into its mom's pouch. She smiled and moved on. Suddenly she heard a bike horn blow behind her. She jumped to the side out of the way. A man riding a bicycle with long legs and an unusually long neck wearing a hat passed them.

Again, Penny looked at the strange person thinking something was extremely odd about them. She shrugged and kept moving along the trail around the zoo. The next enclosure they got to was the ostriches. Penny always thought the ostriches were the funniest birds with their long legs, big body, and how they would put their head into the dirt thinking they were hidden from everybody.

Next, Penny decided to go into the reptile house. It was cool inside, and she saw all kinds of snakes, lizards, spiders, and other creatures she wasn't sure about. Penny didn't really like the reptile house, but you had to go through it to see the otters and seals on the other side.

The same lady that fed the bears had a cart of fish she was throwing to the seals and otters. She saw Penny. "Want to throw some fish."

Penny thought it might be fun but didn't like the smell of the dead fish. "No, thanks, I think I'll pass."

"Okay, have fun."

They walked down some steps and found the panda pen. The pandas were rolling around on a bed of bamboo. Some were eating the bamboo while others were throwing the sticks of bamboo into the air.

Suddenly, Penny, her mom, and her dad were blinded by a light.

"Oh, I'm so sorry, I was trying to get a picture of the pandas playing, but I seemed to have blinded you."

Mom, Dad, and Penny all said, "That's okay."

Penny looked at the person who took their picture. It was the same person as the very tall old lady and the man riding the bike.

"Mom, Dad?"

"What is it, dear?"

"The very tall old lady, the man is riding the bike, and the person is taking the picture...."

"Yes?"

"All of them are the giraffe!!!"

"Really?"

"Yes, look."

"Penny, you are right."

They ran to find the zookeeper. The zookeeper looked at the person hiding behind the camera.

"You are absolutely right. You have found the giraffe. Thank you so much."

The zookeeper gave Penny a huge ribbon, balloons, popcorn, and free admittance into the zoo for one year.

Penny smiled brightly. "Thank you."

The best part of Penny's trip was the pictures of her feeding the bears that mom had taken.

11

THE LOST KEY

This story begins in the wee hours of the morning. It was about three o'clock in the morning when Doris and Darlene woke up. Darlene was an extremely light sleeper, but she was so excited about going to the beach the next day that she hadn't eaten dinner, and now she couldn't sleep.

The girls had to share a bedroom because Doris was too scared to sleep in a room by herself. She talked and snored while sleeping, too. Many nights they kept each other awake all night giggling and laughing until mom came and told them to go to sleep. The girls had tried to stay awake all night, but they had a busy day shopping for beach clothes and accessories that they had fallen asleep by the time they laid their heads on their pillows.

Now that they were once again awake, they wondered if the morning was ever going to show up. Since they couldn't sleep anyway, they decided to go into their playroom to play quietly until mom and dad got up and got ready to leave. They each put on their slippers and eased down the stairs; they remembered to step over the creaky board on the fourth step of the staircase since they didn't want to wake their parents.

When they got to the bottom of the stairs, they eased down the hall and stood still outside the door to their playroom. "I don't think we woke them. Come on." Darlene said, motioning Doris to come into the playroom.

The girls eased into the room and quietly closed the door. They chose a puzzle and spread the pieces out onto the floor. They had just gotten the outside edges put together when they heard a strange noise coming from the far side of the room.

Doris whispered, "What's that noise?"

Darlene looked around, trying to see if she could figure out where the noise was at. "It sounds like somebody crying."

Darlene walked over toward one corner of the room, where an old rocking chair sat. On the floor beside the rocking chair sat a rag doll. She was facing their doll house. Her hair was long and blonde and had been tied up in pigtails with shiny purple bows. She was wearing a purple dress with pink spots and on her feet were the darkest purple shows Darlene had ever seen.

The doll was crying large crocodile tears. They were trailing down her rosy cheeks and splashing on her pretty purple dress.

The girls didn't see she had something on her lap at first, but as they got closer, they saw a small brown wiener dog lying on her lap. He looked very scared and dirty. He began shaking violently as the girls got closer to him.

Doris asked shyly, "Why are you crying? Who are you?"

The doll turned around slowly until she was facing the girls. She was holding the tiny brown dog in her arms. She jumped up and stared at the girls.

"I'm Chrissy, and I came to life tonight under the light of the new moon. This only happens once a year during the Summer Solstice. This year, the new moon brought my dog to life, too, but it didn't work right on him."

"Why didn't it work right on him?"

"Well, you see, my dog is a wind-up dog, and the new moon's light didn't get rid of that feature. I seemed to have lost his key, and now he can't walk or talk. All he does is lay here and shiver because he is so scared."

"Does your dog have a name?"

"Well, yes, his name is Pop-Tart."

. . .

"How can we fix Pop-Tart?"

"We must take Pop-Tart to Mother Nature."

"Mother Nature? How do we find Mother Nature?"

"We have to use magic, of course."

Doris laughed, "Magic isn't real."

"You think so?" Chrissy asked. Chrissy started rubbing her left shoe with her left hand and pointed toward the puzzle the girls had been working on. Instantly, all the puzzle pieces began floating around in the air. The girls watched as the puzzle put itself together while in the air. Chrissy slowly brought her finger down, and the puzzle floated to the floor, still put together.

"Now do you believe that magic is real?" asked Chrissy.

"That was awesome!" exclaimed Doris. "Yes, I believe magic is real."

Darlene spoke up, "Now that you have shown us that magic is real, could you tell us how we can find Mother Nature so we can help Pop-Tart?"

. . .

"Well, everyone gather around and hold hands." All the girls held hands. "Now, close your eyes."

Doris and Darlene closed their eyes tight and held on to each other. In what seemed like a blink of an eye, Chrissy said, "Open your eyes."

When Doris and Darlene opened their eyes, they were standing in a golden room that was adorned with all kinds of gems and jewels. The girls were looking around in awe. They jumped when they heard a golden voice.

"Hello, girls, what has brought you to my house?"

"It is Pop-Tart, the wind-up dog. He was turned into a real-life dog in the new moon's light, but it didn't work right. Can you fix him?" Chrissy asked.

"Let me see what went wrong."

Chrissy handed Pop-Tart to Mother Nature. She held the tiny dog in her hands. She bent down and kissed his head. She smiled and placed the little dog on the floor. Pop Tart immediately went running toward Chrissy.

. . .

Chrissy scooped him up. "He can run!! Thank you, Mother Nature!"

"You are most welcome, Chrissy. Here's an extra wind-up key encase this happens again. Plus, I'm going to give each of you an extra key, too."

The girls all thanked Mother Nature and started to leave.

"You have a very long journey ahead of you, and you all look so tired; why don't you sleep here with me tonight?"

The girls were too tired to argue. They followed Mother Nature to a beautiful bedroom with fluffy pillows and blankets. The girls climbed into bed and were asleep in no time.

When Doris and Darlene woke the next morning, they were both in their beds, nice and neat. They opened their hands, and tucked inside were wind-up keys for Pop-Tart. They looked at each other and jumped out of bed. They went running downstairs and burst into their playroom. There, in a stream of sunlight, lay Chrissy the doll with Pop-Tart lying beside her. They each tried their key in Pop-Tart, and he barked and ran around the room. Darlene picked up Chrissy and placed her on a bed inside the doll house. She gave her a quick kiss. Doris waited for Pop-Tart to wind down before she picked him up. She placed him in the house beside Chrissy.

.　.　.

"Come on, girls, we need to leave soon." Mom and Dad yelled from the kitchen.

"Coming," they said. They looked down at Chrissy and Pop-Tart again, and both the dog and the doll winked up at the girls. The girls smiled at each other, placed Pop Tart's keys in a small box, and placed that box on the bookshelf behind their favorite book, Corduroy. They joined hands and walked to the kitchen with their secret.

12

THE MYSTERIOUS DOLL

Cynthia's birthday was in two days, and she was more than excited. This was her last birthday before she turned into a teenager. She was putting the finishing touches on all the decorations. They had to be spooky. Cynthia was born the week before Halloween, and her Aunt Jean, her mom's older sister, had always made a point of getting her spooky gifts that Cynthia's mother hated.

Cynthia's mother had always tried to dress her in frilly, lacy dresses, and Cynthia had always made a point of staining them, tearing them, or "losing" them. Aunt Jean was into the same things as Cynthia, mostly anything that leaned to the spooky. Aunt Jean traveled a lot, but she made sure she made it back for Cynthia's birthday.

Cynthia always loved the gifts that Aunt Jean brought her. Aunt Jean gave Cynthia a shrunken head she had gotten in South America when she went on vacation. This gift caused a big argument between her mom and aunt. Mom was afraid it would give Cynthia nightmares, but it hadn't so far.

Aunt Jean was also a great storyteller. She could tell the creepiest, most interesting stories that Cynthia had ever heard. Cynthia loved Aunt Jean's creepy stories that gave her goosebumps. Her favorite story was one about a beautiful woman wearing a white dress that would hitch a ride with someone at night. The woman never talked but just got in your car when you stopped. Then suddenly, without warning, she would just disappear out of the car. Cynthia's mom verified the story as one coming from Malaysia, and some of her friends had picked up this woman.

Cynthia went to sleep the night before her party with scary stories on her mind. What Cynthia didn't know was she was soon going to be wrapped in a spooky story of her very own.

On the morning of her birthday, Cynthia bounced out of bed and headed into the kitchen to grab a bite to eat. Cynthia threw open the fridge to check on the big bowl of "blood." It had toes, fingers, and eyes floating around in it. Cynthia scooped a cup for herself, but mom said she couldn't have that kind of drink so early in the morning.

"But, mom, it's my birthday," Cynthia whined.

By lunchtime, Cynthia was bouncing all over the house. "Mom! When is Aunt Jean getting here?"

"I'm here now, my ghoulish girl!" Cynthia ran screaming into her Aunt Jean's outstretched arms.

"Where's my present? Where'd you hide it?"

"Can't you wait until your party?"

"NO!! Give it now."

Aunt Jean laughed and handed Cynthia a bag. "Just be careful it's breakable."

Cynthia looked into the bag. "Oh, it's a doll… um… thanks, I guess… did my mom talk to you before you bought this?"

"Hey, you should know me by now; I'm not going to give you just any ordinary doll. Gently take her out and give her a good look. She does have a story that I need to tell."

Cynthia eased the doll out of the bag and held her up. She looked into her big black eyes. The doll was pretty with brown curly hair, long eyelashes, and of course, her black eyes. She did feel creepy, and wait… did her eyes just flash?

"Okay, I get the creepy vibe Aunt Jean. Does she want me to talk to her or what?"

"Just sit down and listen to her story."

"I found her in an antique shop. She seemed out of place among all the dishes, paintings, vases, and other vintage house wares. She was sitting in a basket on a shelf at the back of the store. I was immediately drawn to her. I knew she would be the perfect gift for you. She even comes with a note attached."

"A note? I didn't see a note. What does the note say?"

"Look closely. I didn't read it. I figured since I was buying her for you, you should be the one to read it."

Cynthia began searching the doll and found the note pinned to the back of her dress. "I found it."

"What does it say?"

Cynthia opened the note, and this is what it said: "She is a naughty girl, and naughty girls have to be punished. May she learn her lesson or forever hold her peace." Cynthia immediately felt a weird sensation in the pit of her stomach. "What exactly does this mean?"

"I don't know, but you have to admit this was the perfect gift. Your mom is going to think that I have given you a normal girly gift, but both of us know better, don't we?"

"Yeah, sure…" but deep down, Cynthia wasn't so sure. There was just something strange about the doll, but she just couldn't figure it out…

A few days passed, and Cynthia still couldn't shake the feeling that there was something really strange about her doll. Every time she would go into her room, she swore that the doll was staring at her, almost pleading with her to take it down and play with it. But Cynthia just couldn't get up enough courage to touch the doll. Cynthia dropped her backpack on her bed and took out her homework. Cynthia hated math, and now she had to learn about fractions. Even after listening and watching her teacher show them how to do fractions, she still didn't understand what to do. She opened her math book and looked at all the things on the page. She didn't know how in the world she was going to get through this.

Cynthia tried her best to do the work on the page but knew everything she had done was wrong. She heard her mom call to her to come to dinner, so she left everything and went downstairs to eat. After dinner, it was her turn to help her mom wash the dishes and clean the kitchen. Once they were through, mom asked her if she had finished her homework. Cynthia shook her head and went back upstairs. She knew she had left her math book open, but now it was closed. Cynthia slowly opened her book, and there was her homework done. Cynthia looked around at her doll. She could have sworn that her doll winked at her. Cynthia shook her head in disbelief. It was only her imagination playing tricks on her.

Weeks passed, but Cynthia's feelings about her doll didn't. There were times when she swore that it was looking at her and pleading with her to talk to it, play with it, or something. She would always shake it off as it being her imagination.

On one particular day, mom brought a basket full of Cynthia's laundry into her room. Cynthia was sitting at her desk working on her spelling homework.

"Hey, Cyn, here's your clean clothes."

"Thanks, mom; just put the basket in my closet, and I'll put them away later."

As soon as this came out of Cynthia's mouth, she regretted it. There was a pile of clothes on the floor of her closet that she had been promising her mom that she would put away. When mom opened the door of the closet, she had to jump back as a pile of jeans toppled over onto her feet.

"Cynthia Jean, this pile of clothes better be put away before you go to bed tonight, or you will be grounded until your 13th birthday!"

"But, mom, I have homework to do," whined Cynthia.

"I don't care; you've promised me every week that you were going to put these clothes away. DO IT NOW!"

"Fine!" Cynthia got up from her desk and pretended to be putting away her clothes. She hung up two shirts and then went back to her homework. It wasn't long before mom called her down to dinner.

Once dinner was finished, Cynthia excused herself. "Did you get those clothes put away?"

Cynthia called from the stairs, "Almost finished."

"They better be; I will check before you go to bed."

Cynthia groaned as she trudged back up the stairs. She was glad that she had snuck some cookies out of the kitchen. She opened the door to her room and walked over to her closet. She opened the door and gasped in surprise. All of her clothes had been put away. The shirts had been hung, sweaters folded and placed on the shelf, jeans folded and placed beside the sweaters. Her shoes had even been straightened up and put together at the back of the closet. Her jackets had even been hung on the hooks on the back of her door.

Cynthia looked around at her doll. She walked over to her and picked her up. There was that weird sensation in the pit of her stomach again. Cynthia looked her doll in the eye. She sat down on her bed with the doll propped against her pillows. Cynthia took a cookie out of the napkin she had in her pocket. The doll's eyes lit up when she saw the cookie.

"Do you want a cookie?" Cynthia held out a cookie toward the doll. To Cynthia's surprise, the doll smiled at her. With a shaking hand, Cynthia broke a cookie in half and held the cookie out to the doll. Cynthia watched in amazement as the doll reached for the cookie. The doll silently munched her cookie while watching Cynthia.

"Did you clean my closet and do my math homework?"

The doll slowly blinked her eyes and smiled at Cynthia while reaching for another bite of cookie. Cynthia felt a bit scared, but suddenly everything was perfectly clear to her. The doll wasn't going to hurt her. She would help Cynthia in any way she needed it. All Cynthia had to do was believe in the doll and give her a cookie every day.

13

THE MOON IS MISSING

One night after her mom and dad fall fast asleep, Misha gets her goggles and eases out of her house. Misha loves going to the beach at night because this is where her best friend lives. Misha walks to her normal sitting spot, and she calls out to her friend.

"Rufus, are you here?"

Misha could sit on the shore for hours just watching Rufus flying out of the water and diving back under the waves. You see, Rufus is a flying fish, and he just loves to do tricks and show off his talents.

This particular night, Rufus looked worried. Misha asks him, "What is the matter? You look very upset."

"Don't you see it? The moon is gone."

"What?" Misha looks up, and Rufus is right. Their big beautiful friend is not beaming brightly from the sky. All they could see was a huge hole where she used to be.

"She was there last night! She rose out of the sea in front of us. Could she be lost under the water?"

Rufus says, "We have got to find her!"

"There's no way we can see anything without her light to guide us! What are we going to do?"

Suddenly, Rufus sees something in the water. Each time a wave would break, they saw little sparks of light glowing, and then fading and then glowing and then fading.

"Misha! I have an idea! Climb on my back. We've got to get to those waves!"

Misha climbed onto Rufus' back, and it wasn't long before they were at the lights. Misha put her goggles on and held onto Rufus as tightly as she could. Misha dove under the water and gasped. She felt like she was floating with the stars. She was surrounded by tiny, glowing creatures floating in the sea.

"Wow, what are they?" she whispered to Rufus.

"They are called plankton. They might be able to help give us light as we explore the sea." Rufus said.

Misha swims over to a group of plankton and asks, "Would you share your light with us? The moon is missing, and we need your light to find her."

"You are going to need more than just our light. Let me see if I can find more friends to help."

It wasn't long before Rufus and Misha were joined by thousands of tiny glowing plankton with their flickering lights.

Misha wonders where the moon could be. Misha heard a booming, deep voice close to her ear, "I can help, too."

Misha turned around and saw eight tentacles that belonged to a firefly squid glimmering in the darkness. His body was covered in glowing blue lights.

"I saw the moon go this way a few minutes ago."

Misha was a bit scared of his huge tentacles, but if the firefly squid's lights could help them see better under the water, she would just be careful around them. The firefly squid motioned for Misha to hold on to his tentacles.

"I'm ready," Misha called.

"Hold on tight!"

The firefly squid, the plankton, Rufus, and Misha begin swimming deeper in the sea. They keep going down to where the water is extremely dark. The plankton grew brighter, and the squid began flashing his lights. But they still couldn't see the moon.

They saw an anglerfish while they were looking for the moon. The anglerfish had been looking for something to eat. Misha saw that she had very large teeth that protruded out of her mouth, but Misha was not scared of anything anymore.

"Hello," said Misha. "We are looking for the moon. You haven't seen her have you?"

"Yes, I have. I saw her swimming with the moonfish a couple of hours ago. They went this way."

The plankton, the squid, Rufus, and Misha follow the glowing lure of the anglerfish. All the lights from the animals create a spotlight on the seas' dark floor.

All of a sudden, Misha sees a rock with something white sticking out from under it. It is the moon!

The moon squeaks at the friends, "Help me. I'm stuck."

The squid wrapped a tentacle around the rock and lifted it off of the moon. Everyone shouts, "Hurray!" when the moon slips out from under the rock.

Rufus swims up to the moon. "What happened?"

"I came here to meet the moonfish. They are my cousins, you know. I got lost when I was trying to find my way home, and my light started fading. Then I bumped into this rock, and it rolled on top of me. I've been trying to push it off of me, but since I don't have any hands, that was hard to do. Thank you for not giving up on me and coming to rescue me."

"Is this where you go if you aren't in the sky?" Misha asks.

"Yes," said the moon and started to float up toward the seas' surface. When she reached the surface of the sea, she stopped.

"Have I ever told you the story of how I became beautiful?"

Misha, Rufus, and all the other sea creatures said "no."

"Well, let me tell you my story as I float back into the sky."

Thousands of years ago, I was not as beautiful as I am now. I didn't have my bright, round face that shone a gentle, soft light on the world. But in one night, I was changed. I started out being gloomy and dark, and nobody liked looking at me, and this made me very sad. I began complaining to the stars and flowers because they were the only ones that would even look at me.

I didn't like being the moon. I wanted to be a flower or star. I knew if it was a star, even a tiny star, some wonderful person would take care of me, but I was only the moon, and nobody liked me. I just wanted to be a flower and grow tall and beautiful in someone's garden where beautiful women would come and smell me. They might even pick me and put me in their hair. I was willing to even be a flower in the middle of a forest where nobody would see me, but the birds or forest animals would come sing to me or visit with me, but I was only the moon, and nobody cared.

The stars would talk to me and say: "We can't help. We were born where we are, and we can't move around. We didn't have anybody to help us. We shine brightly every night to make the sky light up. But this is all we are able to do."

The flowers would sweetly smile and say: "We don't know how to help you. We stay in one place in our garden near our beautiful lady who is very kind to us and to everyone she meets. Maybe we can tell her your story and see if she can help."

I was still very sad, but one evening I got the courage to go visit this lovely lady and see if she could help me. This is what I said to her: "Your face is very beautiful. I would like that you would come to me and that my face could look like your face. You move with grace and gentleness. If you would come to me, we could be one and be perfect. Even the meanest people in the entire world would just look at our beauty and would love us. Please tell me how you became so beautiful?"

She turned her face and looked at me. "I have always lived with people who were happy and gentle, and I think this is what creates goodness and beauty."

I would go see this beautiful maiden every night, and when I saw how beautiful and gentle she was, my love grew stronger, and I wanted so much to be like her forever. One day this beautiful maiden went to her mother and asked her, "I want to go live with the moon forever. Would you let me go?"

Her mother didn't think much about this question, so she didn't even give the maiden a reply. So this beautiful maiden told everyone she knew that she would be going to live with me. In just a couple of days, she had left. This shocked her mother, and she looked everywhere for her beautiful daughter. One of the maiden's friends told her mother, "She went to live with the moon. She asked you many times."

Years passed, and nobody could find the beautiful maiden. They finally decided that she had gone to live with me and she would not ever come back. My face is beautiful now. I have a bright, happy face that gives the world a gentle, soft light.

As the moon told her story, she rose higher and higher into the sky. By the time her story was finished, she was back in her spot and shining brightly. Misha and Rufus waved at the moon once she got settled. They then begin swimming back to shore so Misha can go home. Once they reached the beach where their journey began, Misha walked out of the water and onto the shore. She turned and waved at all her new friends beaming in the moonlight.

All the glowing creatures under the sea glowed brightly long into the night.

14

THERE IS SOMETHING WEIRD ABOUT
GRANNY BEAR

Granny Bear was being weird these days. She had been helping the Bear family for a very long time, but it seems like cooking and making beds have made her a bit off her rocker.

It was just small things that the Bear family began noticing. Sometimes their food was too cold or too hot, or it just tasted a bit off. She would sometimes add strange ingredients to their food, like twigs and leaves, when she knew her family loved bananas, bacon, and berries. There were times when she insisted that they didn't go for a walk after dinner but just sat around the fire in their chairs.

"You can't go for a walk today, it's too hot, plus you guys are looking too thin." She would say as she patted the pillows in the chairs.

"It isn't bad trying to be healthy. Walking is very good for the heart." Papa would say.

Granny would look over the rim of her glasses at Papa and shake her head. One morning she began spooning chocolate sauce over their oatmeal. But Mama said to eat it anyway, so we didn't hurt Granny's feelings.

Mama and Papa Bear didn't seem to be too worried about Granny, but I was. I noticed she started growing weird hairs from her nostrils and ears, plus there was a patch right under her chin. I never remembered her having all these long hairs, but nobody else seemed to worry about them.

When I mentioned them to Granny, she would pat me on the head and just say, "People get hairier when you get older."

Papa Bear thought she needed a vacation. Mama Bear thought she should just sit in the garden sipping on a cup of tea. We all agreed that Granny needed to find some hobbies of her own. We tried to show her how to collect stamps. Mama tried to show her how to macramé, but Granny just wouldn't try any of it. She just wanted to feed us and make us sit around the fire.

One day, there was a knock on the door, and to everyone's surprise, there stood a pretty blonde girl wearing a red dress and hooded cloak. She was carrying a basket of goodies with her. Granny Bear scooted the little girl in with a big grey paw.

"What do you have in your basket there, sweetie?"

"I've got an apple pie, a cherry pie, chocolate chip cookies, peanut butter cookies, and oatmeal raisin cookies."

"That sounds yummy! Let's eat!"

The little girl skipped into the kitchen and put all the goodies on the table. Granny had sliced up the pies and divided them all out into five plates. She then proceeded to divide the cookies evenly.

We all ate happily and greedily since Granny had been messing up the food lately. The little girl was plump and lovely; she had rosy cheeks and a sweet smile. Granny Bear kept patting the little girl and commenting on her lovely complexion and her wonderful appetite. The two seemed to be getting very close to each other. Soon all the food that the little girl had eaten got to her, and she yawned. Granny noticed.

"Oh, you poor, sleepy child, why don't you go upstairs and take a nap?"

As I watched them walking up the stairs, things seemed off, but Granny was happy to have this little visitor. This little visitor seemed happy to have a warm bed to sleep off all that food. Granny came back downstairs looking a bit plumper and very smug with herself.

Granny chuckled and stated, "She was such a funny little girl. She decided she didn't want to take a nap."

"Well, where is she?"

"She went home, of course."

"How did she go home? We didn't see her come down the stairs."

"She decided to go out the window."

"She jumped out the window from upstairs?"

"She didn't jump silly; she slid over to the big oak tree right outside my window and climbed down. She waved and said she had to get home."

Mama and Papa Bear shrugged. "We're going for a walk."

"I'm going to stay with Granny."

"Okay, have fun."

I walked over to the window, and there was not a tree anywhere near the house. Now I took the time to take a good hard look at Granny, and she didn't look like Granny Bear at all. As I looked at Granny, her belly did a bit of a wiggle, and I could have sworn that I heard someone scream. Granny excused herself by saying she had forgotten something upstairs. As she climbed up the stairs, her skirt swayed a bit to the side, and I saw a big orange/grey tail swish out from under it.

That tail did not belong to a Granny Bear. It was the kind wolves had!

"Granny!!" I shouted. I knew the Heimlich Maneuver from school, and I ran up the stairs taking two at a time. I found her in her bedroom looking at me in a weird sort of way.

"Why, Baby Bear, what can I do for you?"

I didn't say anything to her; I just ran into the room and gave her the biggest bear hug I had ever given to anyone. I squeezed once, twice, and on the third time, the little girl popped out of the wolf's mouth. I squeezed again, and out popped the real Granny Bear. This was the Granny who knew how to cook all the things I loved.

The Granny Wolf/Bear didn't take the time to explain anything to me or to clean the mess she just threw up. She just ran out of the house on all four legs. Just as Granny rounded the bend in the road, Mama and Papa Bear got back from their walk. They looked at the mess Granny Wolf/Bear left behind and started to get angry with me.

The real Granny Bear put a protective paw out. "Why don't I make a pot of tea, and we go drink it in the garden while I explain what happened and how my Baby Bear saved two lives today."

We had just sat down at the table in the garden with a pot of tea and a plate of cookies when we heard the doorbell ring. The little girl jumped up to go answer the door. From the garden, we all heard her scream. She came running back screaming, "there's a wolf at the door!"

Granny Bear went walking up to the door and peeked out. Granny's eyes weren't all that good, but with her glasses, she could see that it was only the little boy who lived down the lane wearing a pair of pajamas that looked like a wolf.

Granny chuckled and said, "It's only the little boy down the lane wearing a pair of pajamas that look like a wolf."

Granny opened the door. "Hey, what can I do for you?"

"I smelled your tea and cookies. May I have some?"

"Of course, you can; come on out back and join in the fun."

Granny brought the boy out back, and we all ate and drank until there wasn't anything else to partake of. It wasn't long before I, the little girl, and he was playing hide and seek in the garden. All the plants made for wonderful hiding spots, plus it smelled good hiding behind the roses.

For a day that had started off weird, it ended very happily.

15

THE CASE OF THE MYSTERIOUS JACKET

Samuel loved visiting his grandparents. Even though it was a ten-hour drive by car, he would normally get to visit on special occasions like Christmas, Thanksgiving, birthdays, etc. He didn't like that he lived so far away when he was young, but as he got older, he realized that this distance-limited how often he got to visit, and this made the visits a lot more special. He didn't understand why his cousins, who lived just down the street from his grandparents, never wanted to be in their house. As he got older, he began to understand. It was just normal for them to see their grandparents, and they didn't look at it as being special. It was just an ordinary day for them at Grandpa's and Mimi's, where they didn't have any toys, no basketball, and no playing rough. The only television they had was in the living room, where all the other adults were, and they didn't want it to be on. For Samuel, none of this mattered. He would follow his Mimi around the kitchen, helping her in any way he could. He would take his Grandpa another drink if he asked.

His Grandpa was a large man. He stood six feet five inches, and to Samuel, who was just a small boy, Grandpa was the biggest man alive. Grandpa was a retired police officer who used to patrol the neighborhood with his K-9 named Prince. There were times when his Grandpa would allow Samuel to walk with him around the neighborhood, and they would take Prince with them. Samuel felt indestructible when he was with Prince and Grandpa. Everybody they passed, whether they were sitting on their porch, driving by, or just walking, would wave and say hello to Samuel's Grandpa. Most people greeted him as Officer Peters, and Samuel heard this during their walks. All the children would ask if they could pet Prince.

As Samuel got older and thought about these walks, he wasn't so sure if Prince was such a great police dog or if he was just a wonderful companion for Grandpa. Just to be walking with Grandpa, whom he loved so much, and seeing how respectful everyone was of Grandpa, made Samuel even more proud to be called his grandson.

There was one thing about Samuel's grandpa, and that was you would never see him without a cigar in his mouth. Even if the cigar wasn't lit, it would always be in his mouth. There would always be a fat, short end held fast between his teeth on the left side of his mouth. If anyone talked to him, he would just talk back to them out of the right side of his mouth. To Samuel, his grandpa could do anything.

The smell of cigars permeated everything, and smelling one today would bring back all kinds of memories to Samuel's mind. When they were nearing the end of their patrol, they would stop in at the corner bar. Everyone at the bar knew everyone and always made Samuel feel like a "big boy." Anytime they went into the bar, they would always sit at the bar. Grandpa would introduce Samuel to everyone in the bar, and then he would order himself a beer and order Samuel a Coke. The bartender would always bring them their drinks along with a short glass to pour them in. Samuel always tried so hard to get a good head on his glass of Coke. Once they had finished with their drinks, Grandpa would reach for his wallet but very seldom did any money come out of his wallet. Either the bartender would foot the bill, or the man who sat next to them, or someone would take care of the bill. Grandpa and Samuel would go to the door and tell all the people goodbye that they had greeted on their way inside. It wasn't the best place to have a young man in, but the memories Samuel held were priceless.

When Samuel turned ten, he was allowed to spend a whole week with his Grandparents without his parents being there. Samuel was beyond excited to know he would be spoiled by his Mimi with treats and get to walk the neighborhood with Prince and his Grandpa. Samuel knew he would get to stop in at the corner bar a couple of times that week.

This week was a magical one for Samuel, and the days were going by way too fast. The day before Samuel was to go home, his grandpa took him into the attic and opened a huge steamer trunk. He took out an old jacket but surprisingly, it was in wonderful shape. He asked me to put on the jacket. It was too large for Samuel, but Grandpa told him he would someday grow into it. Grandpa told me that his father had given him the jacket after he graduated from school and started his first job. Samuel's father told him that as long as he owned this jacket, he would always have money. Grandpa's father pointed to an inside pocket that had been sewn shut, and he was only to open it if he was in desperate need of what was inside the pocket.

Samuel's Grandpa told him that there were several times over the years that he had owned the jacket that he had thought about opening the pocket. As the years progressed and the jacket started to get a bit tattered, Samuel's grandpa had thought about opening the pocket before he threw out the jacket but then would think about what his father said about passing it on to his children. Unfortunately, Grandpa only had three daughters, and the girls wouldn't ever wear his jacket. His daughters eventually got married, so he thought that maybe one of their husbands would be worthy of this jacket. He did love them but just didn't feel like any of them were worthy of the jacket. Grandpa shared all this with Samuel and told him that he had been thinking long and hard about giving the jacket to him. Grandpa said that the night before Samuel got to his house at the beginning of the week that he had dreamed about Samuel wearing the jacket, and he knew that he had made the right decision.

"Just remember that as long as you have this jacket, you won't ever be broke. You are going to feel like opening the pocket but don't do it unless you absolutely have to. Think of it as a Christmas gift; when it is opened, the mystery will be gone, and there won't be any more anticipation."

This was very hard for Samuel to understand as he was only ten, but as he grew, he began to understand what he had said. There were times in Samuel's life when he thought about opening the pocket, he hoped he would find a fortune so he could buy a new bike or baseball glove, but every time he thought about doing it, he remembered Grandpa's words sitting in that attic. Samuel could not want to be the person to end his great grandfather's mystery, and he wasn't ever in a dire enough situation to warrant it being opened.

As time passed and Samuel retired the jacket from being worn regularly to it getting packed away in his attic, Samuel wrapped the jacket in paper carefully and placed it in the same steamer trunk his Grandpa took it out of. Samuel eventually married and shared this wonderful story with his wife, and she agreed that this mystery wasn't theirs to open. Yes, they had some very hard times with bankruptcy right around the corner, but the pocket remained closed.

Samuel had two daughters, and even though he shared his story with them, they didn't have any interest in wanting the jacket. The jacket remained in storage along with the mystery.

Samuel's daughters eventually got married, and one of them had a son. Samuel wondered if it was time to give this mystery to him. He was getting ready to turn ten in just a couple of months. This was the same age Samuel received the jacket. Samuel decided that he would give his grandson this jacket at his party. Once the day rolled around, and all the other presents had been opened, Samuel asked his grandson to go outside with him. Samuel walked to a big oak tree at the far end of the yard. He handed him a large box that held the jacket, but before Samuel allowed his grandson to open the box, he asked him how he was feeling. His grandson said he felt appreciation and excitement for the unopened, unknown gift. Samuel told him how once he opened this gift, the anticipation and excitement would change, and all the mystery would be known. Samuel told him to open the gift. Samuel's grandson opened the box, and without any words, he looked at his grandpa in a puzzling way.

Samuel then took the time to tell him the long story about how the jacket had come into his possession. Samuel showed his grandson the pocket that had been sewn shut that housed the mystery of the family. Samuel told him that he himself didn't know what was in the pocket as it had never been opened by anyone. Samuel explained that once the pocket was opened, the mystery would stop being a mystery. Samuel asked him if he had any questions. Samuel's grandson gave him a hug and told his Grandpa:

"Grandpa, I will take good care of this jacket and the mystery it holds. Some day I want to give it to my grandson."

Samuel smiled and knew that he had made the right decision to give the jacket to his grandson. The mystery that lived inside Samuel's great grandfather's jacket remained inside that jacket for generations and was never opened. It became clear to the one who had it before they passed it down to the next generation that the mystery wasn't what was within the pocket but instead the encouragement, the strength, the hope, and the story it gave to them.

16

WHAT'S IN AUNT JACKIE'S TRUNK?

There is a light in Aunt Jackie's attic that won't stop flickering. It swings by a dusty cord that hangs from the rafters. It buzzes like the flies in the barn around the cows. Dust travels up my nose. It wants me to get scared, sneeze, and leave.

Aunt Jackie doesn't want anyone up here, but I just have to look around. My shoulders feel heavy, and the air tries to push me away. I have to know if what I have heard is true.

The stairs are so loud. If you listen closely to their groans, you can hear them tell you to leave. The banisters try to shoot splinters into my hand, but nothing will stop me from looking inside that trunk sitting in the corner of Aunt Jackie's attic.

This time I'm going to do it. When I say this time, I mean "third time's the charm."

The first time I tried this, I stayed at the house while everybody else went to Miss Mary's barbecue. I thought I could do three things fast:

One: run up the stairs to the attic.

Two: pick the trunk's lock.

Three: learn the mystery of the trunk.

I really thought I could do this with time to make it to the barbecue before all Miss Mary's potato salad and ribs had been eaten. I was so silly.

The lid to the trunk was completely covered in spider webs. When I touched the lock, a wave of baby spiders swarmed over my hand. I'm sure I screamed, but I can't remember. I'm also sure I left my shorts, socks, and shirt all along the stairs. I just wanted to jump into the shower as quickly as I could.

In spite of my best efforts, I spent the whole weekend itching and jittery. I was convinced that I had spiders living in my hair. When I did make it to Miss Mary's, all that was left was some fruit salad that tasted funny and some burnt hot dogs.

I never told anybody about my first attempt to fight the attic, but I do think that Aunt Jackie knows. I found my shorts, socks, and shirt laundered and folded on the kitchen table the next morning. Aunt Jackie never said anything, but she calls me "Twitch" at times. It might be that she likes secrets.

I have a weird family anyway. Jackie isn't even my aunt's real name. Her real name is Elizabeth. The reasoning behind it is that she couldn't pronounce some words right when she was younger, and instead of saying jacket, she said "Jackie." So everyone started calling her "Jackie." There are only a few things I know to be the truth about Jackie:

One: she has long curly grey hair that always smells like lavender.

Two: she always wears some shade of purple.

Three: aunt Jackie has a secret that her attic is helping her hide.

Aunt Jackie's attic is really alive. I can hear it breathing at times when I am sleeping in my room right below the attic. I can heal the thumps and creaks above me. I can feel the roof exhale and inhale when there is a storm brewing. I feel it shudder when the wind blows cold. I can hear boxes moving around up there when there isn't anybody up there.

If you don't believe me about my Aunt Jackie, just visit anyone in Patter County about my Aunt Jackie's attic; there are all kinds of secrets and whispers about Aunt Jackie. They whisper about her unusual strength. They whisper about her wrestling with bobcats. They whisper about all the friends she has made in the woods and the gifts they brought her.

The next time I decided to fight Aunt Jackie's attic, I waited until the early morning hours when everyone was asleep, and Aunt Jackie's snores were heard everywhere. Many people don't like snoring, but I do. If she is snoring, she can't hear me. If she is snoring, she can't see me. If she quits snoring, I know I have to run like crazy back to my room.

I honestly thought that with Aunt Jackie inside, I wouldn't be as afraid of what I had to do. I did think I knew all the answers. I put thick gloves on my hands and duct-taped them to my sleeves. I taped the legs of my jeans to the tops of my slippers. I did all this to keep the spiders from getting into my clothes. I was thinking that wearing the slippers wouldn't make any noises on the stairs. The gloves were to protect my hands from splinters.

I had a paperclip in my right hand to pick the lock with, and I had a broom in my left hand to use as a sword. I had almost thought of everything. The weather even seemed to be with me that night. The thunder and winds made the house creakier, and this made my footsteps a lot harder to hear. I was also too confident. I completely forgot about the window that was missing a pane in the attic.

If you were looking at the attic from the outside, the missing pane looked like a missing tooth. But the most important thing I forgot was that wild animals like to take shelter from the storm inside attics if they can find a way in.

Because of the snores, wind, and storm, I made it all the way up the stairs before I noticed any movements over my head. The bats didn't get inside my clothes because of the duct tape, but I did lose my paperclip and broom during my quick retreat. Nobody is allowed in the attic, but I just have to know.

I have to know if all the rumors and whispers are true. But now I am smarter, and there are three things I know:

One: it will be different this time.

Two: I am ready this time.

Three: ...

There is a light in Aunt Jackie's attic that won't stop flickering. It swings by a dusty cord that hangs from the rafters. It buzzes like the flies in the barn around the cows. Dust travels up my nose. It wants me to get scared, sneeze, and leave.

Aunt Jackie doesn't want anyone up here, but I just have to look around. My shoulders feel heavy, and the air tries to push me away. I have to know if what I have heard is true.

The stairs are so loud. If you listen closely to their groans, you can hear them tell you to leave. The banisters try to shoot splinters into my hand, but nothing will stop me from looking inside that trunk sitting in the corner of Aunt Jackie's attic.

Not after the last time...

17

THE MYSTERIOUS HOUSE

Seth and Brittany were so excited. Tonight was Halloween, and they were getting to go Trick-or-Treating by themselves for the first time. When mom opened the front door and told them to be careful, they quickly ran down the steps and disappeared up the street.

Brittany had decided to dress up as Red Riding Hood. She was wearing a red cape with a hood and carried a basket to put her goodies in instead of a normal basket. She also had her favorite stuffed dog with her for the "big bad wolf," Marmaduke. Seth decided to be the fastest person he knew. He had saved his money and bought a Flash costume.

All the roads were full of children in fantastic costumes carrying plastic bags, plastic pails, and baskets. There were some older children, too, but most of these were just chaperones for a little sister or brother. Seth and Brittany even saw some of their friends along the way. They complemented each other's costumes and went on their way.

As the evening wore on, Seth and Brittany went to more and more houses until they reached some of the more out-of-the-way places within their neighborhood. They hadn't been able to walk this far last night while they were out looking at all the houses they wanted to go to. Brittany stopped quickly. The candy inside her basket rustled in protest when she stopped so suddenly. She grabbed Seth by the arm. Seth looked at where she was pointing. She was pointing to a house that looked like it was empty.

"I don't remember this house from last night, do you?"

Seth looked at the house and started questioning himself as to whether or not he had seen that house last night. He knew he walked by that street when they went to school, so he must have noticed it, but now he wasn't so sure.

The house they were looking at looked time-worn and weary. Rather than it having grass that was cut neatly, there were only weeds growing. They couldn't see any lights shining from the inside, so they figured it was empty. Both children felt curious but also scared. They looked at each other and knew what the other was thinking. They nodded to each other and walked up to the house.

The wooden boards on the front porch creaked and groaned in protest as they stepped onto it. The door was covered in cobwebs, and Seth had to pull some off of the door knob. He tentatively turned the knob, and to his surprise, it turned and opened. The door screeched in protest as it opened slowly. They didn't get inside the house when something popped up in their faces and said: "Hello!"

They got away from that house as quickly as they could. They screamed until they stopped. Once they knew they were far away enough from that house, they stopped to catch their breath. Brittany's heart was beating so fast that she thought it might jump out of her chest. Seth was standing bent over with his hands on his knees. He stood up and asked Brittany if she was okay.

"Yes, but I think we should go home."

"Okay, but where did you leave, Marmaduke?"

Brittany looked around her. She looked in her basket. "Oh, no, I've dropped Marmaduke. I bet he's at the house."

They looked at each other, knowing that they would have to go back to that creepy house and get Marmaduke. Once they got back to the house, they tiptoed up to the door and made sure that they didn't make any noise that would tell anyone inside that they were there. They looked on the front porch but didn't see Marmaduke anywhere. Somebody behind them asked: "Is this what you are looking for?"

They slowly turned around but couldn't move at what they saw. He appeared to be a young boy. He was wearing a pair of blue trousers and a red and blue plaid shirt. Instead of having a belt, he was wearing suspenders to keep his pants up. He looked like a normal boy, but he had a pumpkin where his head should have been.

Seth grabbed a chair that was close to him. He was ready to fight with it if he had to. Brittany scurried behind her brother.

"Give me Marmaduke, or I'll hit you with the chair. I am not joking," Seth said with a shaky voice.

"I – I don't mean you any harm. Here's your toy." He said. He kept his arms out in front just to show them that he didn't mean them any harm. He walked a bit closer and placed Marmaduke a few feet in front of them. He then slowly back away. Seth reached down and grabbed Marmaduke. He handed him to

Brittany, and she immediately hugged the dog tightly to her chest.

Since they had gotten Marmaduke back, Seth and Brittany wanted to leave. They moved slowly forward, with Seth still holding the chair in front of him to protect them. He stopped at the bottom of the steps. Even though he wanted to leave as quickly as possible, he was also filled with curiosity, and he just had to ask: "What happened to your head?"

The boy with the pumpkin head looked a bit puzzled, like he didn't quite understand what Seth had asked. There were a few minutes of silence before Seth asked: "Why do you have a pumpkin for a head?"

"Oh, yes, I guess my head is a bit strange to you. Why don't you come inside and I will tell you all about it. We can have some chocolate milk and cookies," he said. He walked toward the door. When he got to the door, he turned around to see if his visitors were following him. "By the way, my name is Jeff."

Seth wanted nothing more than to go home, but he also wanted to know more about Jeff. Before Seth knew what was happening, Brittany had walked past him and was almost to the front door. Seth tried to talk her out of it, but she was already inside, so he just put the chair down and walked in behind her.

Even though the house looked decrepit on the outside, it was very clean inside. There were soft lights glowing in the living room, and the fireplace had it warm and cozy. Seth and Brittany sat down on the couch, and it was surprisingly comfortable and soft.

Jeff had gone off into the kitchen but soon came back with a tray. On the tray were two glasses filled with chocolate milk, and there were all kinds of cookies, too. Jeff put the tray in front of Seth and Brittany and told them to eat what they wanted.

During the time Seth and Brittany were eating, Jeff told his interesting story.

Jeff was created by a little boy named Barry. Barry and his family had lived in the house they were sitting in right now. This was many, many years ago. Barry didn't have any friends and was extremely lonely. On one Halloween night, Barry had wanted to go trick-or-treating but didn't have anyone to go with him. So he took the pumpkin he was supposed to be turning into a Jack-O-Lantern and made a wish on a shooting star. The star heard his plea, and it brought Jeff to life. Barry was the one who gave Jeff his name.

They both had fun trick-or-treating that Halloween. Jeff had so much fun with Barry that Halloween that he decided Halloween would be his favorite day. When the next morning rolled around, Barry and his parents were gone. The house was totally empty. Jeff had been waiting on Barry to come back since that day.

Seth and Brittany felt so sorry for Jeff. Seth was very sorry that he had threatened Jeff. Jeff wasn't scary. He was just a lonely and sad boy. Jeff noticed that Seth and Brittany looked very sad. Jeff decided he didn't want to celebrate a gloomy Halloween. He stood up and walked over to the radio. "Let's listen to some Halloween music."

Jeff turned on the radio and began to dance. He motioned for Seth and Brittany to join him. They were a bit hesitant but watching Jeff dance looked like a lot of fun. So they decided to dance with him. They all danced until they were too tired o move.

Time passed quickly. Seth and Brittany realized it was getting late, and they needed to get home. Their parents might start worrying about them if they don't get home soon. Jeff walked them to the door and said their goodbyes. They both gave Jeff some of their candy before they left, and he accepted it gladly. They all waved goodbye before Seth and Brittany made their way home.

Seth and Brittany were both up before their parents the next morning. They decided to run to Jeff's house to see him again. They knocked, but nobody answered the door. They called Jeff's name, but he still didn't appear. They tried the doorknob, and it turned easily. They went into the house and found a pumpkin on top of the table. There was a note on top of the pumpkin. It simply read: "Until next Halloween."

Seth and Brittany left Jeff's house feeling a bit sad that they wouldn't be able to see Jeff for one whole year. They kept Jeff's not and looked at it as a promise between the three friends. They went home and couldn't wait for Halloween to come around again. They knew that they would quickly do some trick-or-treating and then go to Jeff's house to have some real fun.

18

THE CASE OF THE QUARTZ EGGS

The ruined castle was easy to find; all you had to do was follow the path behind Gary's house, go passed the chicken coop, climb over the piles of rocks, and then through a thicket of briars. The briars cleared, and the space that opened made you feel like you were on top of the world.

From this vantage point, you could see the river flowing bluish-green and lapping at the shore. To the right of the river sat a little town. Its buildings were staggered like teeth. To the left of the river were an empty field and a camp ground.

They were so far away that Gary felt like they were just visions. They could have existed from where he was standing. From here, the cars could honk, but he wouldn't hear it. Even the bees buzzing couldn't be heard, but Gary knew there were bees close by because he could smell their honey from where he was standing. For Gary, the ruined castle was a guard tower that sat above all these things that didn't seem real. You could not hear anybody call your name up here, so it was almost like homework that didn't exist, and you absolutely did not have to go home to eat lunch if you couldn't hear anyone call you. The ruined castle couldn't be penetrated as its walls were thick.

Gary ran up to the walls of the castle; his legs began stinging where he had run through stinging nettles along the path. He knocked a secret knock, and his friend Bonnie stuck her head out of the door.

"Hey, look, I've found something," Bonnie said.

She held her hand out, and in t was a beautiful piece of quartz in the shape of an egg. It had tiny blue lines going through it, and it looked like it could have been molded because it looked so perfect. Gary gasped.

"Where did you find that?"

"In the corner of a room at the back of the castle. I thought we could clean the room up where we could get if it started raining when we were here. I moved all those branches, twigs, and leaves." Gary looked at all the stuff that Bonnie had moved.

Inside the room, it was partially covered by remnants of the roof, or maybe it was just the floor. It was extremely old, so it was hard to tell what it used to be. But where Bonnie had cleaned the floor, it was beautiful. All the things that had fallen through the roof were gone. Now it looked like an actual house, a little house that belonged to them. Gary was very impressed.

Bonnie stated confidently, "I moved this rock and found this...."

Bonnie waved Gary over to the other side of the room, and Gary saw it. It was a hole that a small child would be able to crawl through, well, if they were brave. Gary gasped and fell to his knees and hands. He had his cheek on the floor and was trying to see what was at the other end. It was too dark for him to see anything. There was just enough light to show that the tunnel went on for a while, and then it turned to the left.

"This is where I found the egg," Bonnie said. "I think it is a dragon egg."

Gary laughed, "Dragons don't exist."

"I have heard about dragon's eggs. They are a type of egg where if you crack them open, you will find crystals in them."

Gary was interested in finding crystals. He sat down and thought for a moment.

"What makes you think there are more inside?"

"Well, I found this one at the edge of the tunnel, and I think that there is another one over there." Bonnie pointed to the other side of the tunnel.

Gary was afraid of tight spaces. He wouldn't even wear a hat or scarves that made him feel like he was being squeezed. When he was at a friend's house, and they would make a sheet fort, he pretended that other games were more interesting but having his very own dragon egg was also exciting.

"Do you want to try to get it?" He asked with a shaky voice.

"I have already tried. But the tunnel is too small for me. You are smaller, so you would probably fit."

Gary's stomach churned, but he looked at the egg in Bonnie's hand and asked to hold it. When he was holding it in his hand, he knew then that he had to have one of his very own. He knew if he had his very own dragon egg, he would put it in his pocket and carry it everywhere he went. It felt like it might be magical. Gary stood up and removed his jacket.

"Hold this; I'm going in."

When he put his knees against the cold floor, he felt as if his heart was going to burst out of his chest; he was so scared that he almost couldn't breathe. When he put his head under the low stone roof, he felt it pressing against him. He felt like the tunnel was squeezing him. He imagined the tunnel had jagged teeth, and he was crawling into its mouth. He concentrated on making his hand and legs move and visualizing holding a dragon's egg in his hand.

Once he got to the place where the egg lay, he noticed something that took his breath. Just beyond the bend of the tunnel, there was a large pile of dragon eggs. They were on the far side of the tunnel. It might have been six feet away. Somewhere there was a light gleaming, and inside the tunnel, it looked like pearls piled on top of each other, just waiting for Gary to grab them with his hands. Within the same moment, he heard a cry that was not human, and he knew deep down that it wasn't his friend Bonnie.

He heard the sound again, and he knew it was coming from the spot where the eggs were. It sounded like a howl, and this echoed down the tunnel chamber, so it was hard for Gary to figure out where exactly it was coming from. Gary was also aware of a wet and pungent smell that wasn't coming from him. Gary knew that some enclosed places would hold stale puddles and bats, but this was something animalistic that didn't want to share their dragon's eggs with small children trapped in a small space.

Gary's heart began beating in his ears. He reached out to see if he could reach any of the eggs without having to go further into the tunnel, but they were just out of his reach. He heard the horrible sound again. This howl bounced off the rocks this time, and Gary knew it was an actual dragon.

He was inside the dragon's home. He knew that now. He should have realized it earlier. There were clues that should have told him. The eggs, the howling, and scratching. Gary felt something cold pass by him. His hair stood up on its ends. He tightly gripped the egg he had already grabbed and decided to get out of the tunnel as fast as he could. He did not want to come face to face with an actual dragon, even if the big pile of eggs was beckoning him to take them so he could treat them like jewels to be admired and loved.

Gary had just started moving backward when the dragon made another cry, and something about its tone made him stop. He didn't move; his skin was tingling, his heart was beating wildly, and he was listening to everything around him. When he heard the sound again, Gary knew he wasn't wrong. The dragon was hurt.

Gary couldn't swallow. He was trapped and didn't want to move. But he knew deep down that he wouldn't ever leave an animal that was hurt. He heard all sorts of sadness in its howls. As if to show just how pitiful it was, he felt a blast of hot air come into the tunnel.

With his heart beating in his throat, he started crawling toward the dragon. The dragon whined. Gary peered around a corner, and he saw the dragon, but it didn't look like a dragon he had imagined or read about. It was furry, fat, and sprawled on top of a pile of stones.

When Gary got closer and realized it wasn't a dragon but their teacher's dog. The dog looked up, and Gary realized it had fallen through the ceiling, and it couldn't move. The dog whimpered as Gary inched toward him. Gary petted the dog, and the dog licked his face in relief. The dog was a lot more scared than Gary was.

Gary pushed himself up through the hole in the ceiling that the dog had fallen through. He surprised Bonnie, who had been digging around in front of the castle. They took the dog to

Bonnie's home, and her mother called its owner, who came and got it.

A few days later, Gary and Bonnie went back to the ruined castle and gathered all the eggs, and put them in a pile in their new playroom. Bonnie suggested they split one, and they both decided to. They used a large rock and broke one egg into two pieces. There wasn't anything inside the egg but a stone that was white and had blue lines running through it, just like the outside.

Gary suggested that they not break anymore open. "I think they look better when they are whole."

So the other 15 eggs stayed in their playroom in the castle forever to be admired by anyone who dared search the castle ruins.

19

IS THE TOOTH FAIRY REALLY A MOUSE?

Loretta has a very loose tooth. It wobbles with every word she says. It is actually causing her to slur her words because she is afraid she will push it out with her tongue. She is standing in front of the bathroom mirror, looking at her loose tooth.

"Is it still hanging on?" asked Mom.

"Yes, I wish it would fall out today."

"Maybe it will, and then the tooth fairy will come to leave you some money."

Loretta goes on to school with her very wobbly tooth. At lunch, she sits beside her best friend, Dottie. She smiles at Dottie, and her tooth wobbles at her best friend.

"I see it is still hanging in there."

"Yes, I don't think it is ever going to fall out."

"It will, and then the tooth mouse will come and bring you a gift."

"The tooth mouse? I haven't ever heard of the tooth mouse."

"Yes, he is very famous in my hometown of Argentina. We call him Raton Diente. He will leave gifts as long as you leave him some water."

Dottie smiles a big smile with both of her front teeth missing.

"So what did Raton Diente leave you for your teeth?"

Dottie pointed to the hole on the left. "For this one, I got a new book. For this one, I got a stuffed animal."

"Wow, those are great gifts."

"Yep."

Their conversation quieted as they shared their lunches as they did every day. Loretta kept wiggling her tooth with her tongue for the rest of the day. Every chance she got, Loretta was wiggling that tooth. She couldn't wait for either the tooth fairy or Raton Diente to come to visit her.

At dinner that night, Loretta's mom asked her if her tooth had fallen out yet. Loretta answered by opening her mouth and wiggling her very loose tooth with her tongue.

"It shouldn't be too much longer now," said mom.

"Probably not, but I have a bigger problem than my loose tooth."

"What kind of problem?"

"Well, Dottie says that the tooth fairy is actually a tooth mouse. That goes by the name of Raton Diente."

"Ah, Dottie, what else did Dottie say?"

Loretta twirled some spaghetti onto her fork before she spoke. "Well, Raton Diente doesn't leave any money; he will leave you a gift as long as you leave him some water."

Mom smiled at Loretta. "Well, maybe they work together."

"Maybe. Do you think that Raton Diente only speaks Spanish?"

"I think Raton Diente and the tooth fairy speak all the languages so they can communicate will all the children of the world."

"That would be cool!"

When Dottie and Loretta met for lunch the next day, Dottie asked, "Is your tooth out yet?"

"Almost; it is wobbly enough to fall out today, I hope."

"If it does, make sure you leave Raton Diente some water."

The girls moved closer to each other so they could whisper. They loved swapping things in their lunches.

Loretta said, "My mom thinks that the tooth fairy and Raton Diente work together."

"That's an interesting suggestion," Dottie said as she broke off half of her turkey wrap and handed it to Loretta. "Why don't we write them a letter to find out?"

"That's a good idea. I can put it under my pillow with the tooth and hope they leave a response with the money or gift, whichever it may be."

When school was out, the girls ran to Dottie's house to write the letter. Loretta grinned with her wobbly tooth still hanging there. "We'll paint some fairy and mouse pictures to make the letter look good."

They tried to hurry because Loretta could feel her tooth getting wobblier and wobblier every time she talked.

"Let's not make it like a letter, but more like a list of questions they need to answer."

"Okay, let's put a "yes" or "no" box after each question."

Here are the questions they asked:

"Does the tooth fairy work with Raton Diente? Yes / No

"Do both of you speak Spanish or other languages? Yes / No

"Do you help a child if they are scared to go to the dentist? Yes / No

"What do you do with all the teeth you take?"

When they finished their letter, it happened. Loretta's tooth fell out right on top of the letter.

Loretta said, "Perfect timing."

Both girls laughed. "We shall see who comes in the morning."

Loretta hurried home to show her mom that her tooth had finally fallen out. Her mom helped her wrap it in a piece of tissue and place it under her pillow with the letter. Loretta put a small bowl of water on her nightstand just in case.

It was hard for Loretta to go to sleep that night, but she finally drifted off to sleep, dreaming of fairies and mice and mice dressed up as fairies. When her alarm clock went off the next morning, she jumped out of bed and moved her pillow. Her tooth was gone. Where it had been was a brand new box of crayons and a crisp dollar bill. Loretta grabbed the letter to see if it had been answered. It has the smallest squiggles on it that it was hard for Loretta to read. Loretta looked at the bowl of water, and it had been drunk dry.

Loretta sat on her bed to read the letter:

"Does the tooth fairy work with Raton Diente?" Yes / No

"We have a large team; there are a lot of children in the world."

"Do both of you speak Spanish or other languages?" Yes / No

"It is very helpful to be able to speak many languages."

"Do you help a child if they are scared to go to the dentist?" Yes / No

"Yes, we help dentists, and don't forget the rules... brush your teeth two minutes every morning, at lunch, and then at bedtime."

"What do you do with all the teeth you take?"

"That is our biggest secret. Look at all the tiny stars in the sky. Look at all the white pebbles along the edge of the sea. Think about all the shiny pearl necklaces for magical mice and fairies. That is all we can tell you."

Loretta and Dottie looked at the letter during lunch while they nibbled on sandwiches, carrot sticks, and chips. Dottie held up the letter. "I still think it was your mom."

"I thought that too, but it isn't my mom's handwriting. She writes big and scratchy, not small and squiggly."

The girls kept looking at the letter and wondering who could have answered it. Dottie bit into a carrot stick.

"Well, we will just have to try again soon. I just got another loose tooth. This time I will stay awake all night."

20

THE PROBLEM WITH ELEVATORS

I n an old building lived a very old elevator. This elevator was extremely small and could only carry three people at one time. Leonard had just turned ten, and he had felt extremely nervous from the very day that his family had moved into their apartment. He had always been uncomfortable riding elevators because he was scared that they would stop between or a cable would break, and he would be sent plummeting to his death. But there was something about this particular elevator that didn't sit well with Leonard. Maybe it was the dirty walls. Maybe it was the door that never wanted to stay open but a few seconds, and then it would slam shut with a loud bang. Maybe it was how the elevator would shudder every time it took off like it was too tired. Perhaps it was just too small. It was crowded with just one person on it.

Leonard thought the stairs were better. He had tried them after school one day. There weren't any windows or lights, and he could hear his footsteps echoing behind on the concrete like there was someone else climbing up behind him. By the time he got to his floor, which was the 17th, he was breathing heavily.

Leonard's father worked from home, and he asked him why he was breathing heavily. When Leonard told him, he asked, "Why don't you take the elevator?"

Leonard hated the look on his father's face. It was always saying you are not just bad at sports; you are weak, skinny, and a coward. From that day on, Leonard would take the elevator. He tried his best to get used to it, just like he got used to being bullied at school.

The problem was that he couldn't get used to it. He was terrified that it would stop between floors, and he would get trapped inside. Even if he rode it with others, he didn't feel any better. He didn't like being close to other people. He didn't like how people tried not to look at each other and just stared at the floor, ceiling, or nothing.

Leonard was riding the elevator down to go to school one morning when the elevator stopped on the 14th floor. The doors opened, and a large lady stepped in. She had on a blue coat that pooled around her feet. As she got onto the elevator, Leonard felt sure it sunk under her tremendous weight. She was so large that her coat brushed against him, and he had to back himself into the corner and hold his breath. There wasn't any room for anybody else. The door closed behind her, and rather than facing the door like everyone else; she turned around to face Leonard.

He looked up at her for a minute before he diverted his eyes back to the floor. She had huge cheeks but no chin. There was just a large mass of skin that was her neck. Her eyes were a very pale blue, almost white, and they were tiny and sharp. Leonard felt as if they were boring holes into his face.

Leonard kept looking at the floor, but the woman never turned around. She just kept staring at him. He looked up quickly to see if she was still looking at him, and she was. Leonard so wanted to turn and face the wall, but there wasn't any room in the elevator for him to do so. The elevator slowly creaked its way down to the first floor. The lady never took her eyes off of Leonard. Surely she was crazy; why else would she constantly stare at him? The lady didn't do anything to Leonard; she just watched him. Once the elevator landed on the first floor, Leonard wanted nothing more than to run out, but she was blocking his way. He had to wait until she turned around and slowly moved off the elevator. Once he was able to, Leonard ran off the elevator and didn't stop until he was at school. He didn't care what anyone thought.

Leonard couldn't get this woman off of his mind all day. He wondered if she lived in the building. He hadn't ever seen her before today, and the building wasn't that big. She might have been visiting someone, but at 7:30? That was way too early to go visiting.

Leonard got nervous once he was back at his building. Why was he so afraid of this old woman? He was ashamed of himself. He pressed the button and got on the elevator. He hoped that it wouldn't stop anywhere along the way. But to Leonard's dismay, it stopped on the fourth floor. Leonard watched the door open, and all he could see what a huge green coat, ice-blue eyes, and that pig of a face staring at him. It was like she knew he was going to be on the elevator. Leonard moved into the corner so she could get her huge body into the elevator. He watched as her hand pushed the button for the 18th floor. Leonard wondered why she got on the elevator at 14 this morning, on at four this afternoon but was getting off at 18?

When the elevator stopped on the 17th floor to let Leonard out, he regretted letting her know what floor he lived on. He had wanted to push a different button but didn't want to touch her.

Leonard said, "excuse me," but the lady barely moved out of his way. He had to squeeze past her. Her coat scratched him as he squeezed by. He was scared that the doors would shut before he could get off. She watched his every move as he got out of the elevator.

Leonard slowly walked to his apartment, knowing there wasn't anything he could do now. At least she didn't know which apartment he lived in. That night at dinner, he asked his father if he had ever noticed a strange lady before?

"Not that I've noticed."

"Well, this lady rode the elevator with me twice today. She just stared at me the whole time. She never quit looking at me for a second."

"Why are you so worried about her?" his father replied, turning away from his television show. "What can I do with you? You are now scared of an old lady."

"I'm not scared."

"Yes, you are. When are you going to stop being scared all the time?"

Leonard didn't want his father to see him cry, so he stood up and went to his room. His dad probably knew he was crying, but there wasn't anything he could do about it. He didn't sleep well that night.

The next morning when Leonard pushed the elevator button, and it stopped on his floor, the lady was already inside the elevator. He just stood there. He couldn't move, then he slowly began backing up. When she noticed Leonard, the look on her face changed. She had a weird smile on her face when the door slammed shut.

Leonard began running down the stairs. They were very dark, and he fell. He broke his leg but managed to crawl back to his apartment to get his dad. His dad didn't say anything on the way to the hospital, but he could feel the disappointment radiating off from his dad. When they got back home, Leonard didn't have a choice now but to ride the elevator because he had to use crutches. At least Leonard would get some relief from the lady, his dad was on the elevator with him, and there wasn't any room for the lady.

On the way up to their apartment, his dad pressed the button for the tenth floor.

"Why did you press 10?"

"I promised Mrs. Rodgers that I would visit with her today."

"I'll go too."

"No, you need to go to your room and get off your leg."

Leonard knew there wasn't any use in arguing with his dad. He watched as his dad got off and headed down the hallway. Leonard quickly pressed 17 again, hoping to make it home without seeing the lady, but unfortunately, the elevator stopped on 11. There stood the lady just like she was waiting for him. She stepped in fast, and Leonard couldn't hobble out of the elevator fast enough. The door closed, and he was trapped.

"Hello, Leonard." The lady looked at Leonard, laughed, and then turned the key to stop the elevator. She opened her large green coat, and Leonard screamed.

CHECK OUT MYSTERY STORIES FOR KIDS PART 1

Check out Part 1 on if you have not already!

Mystery Short Stories for Kids Part 1

Please do not forget to review this book on Amazon if you can spare the time!

Thank You

Made in the USA
Monee, IL
13 September 2022

13885753R10072